THE GIRL
FROM DONEGAL

And Other Short Stories

E. B. McKee

Publisher's Information

EBookBakery Books

Author contact: genem1@cox.net

ISBN: 978-1-938517-92-1
1. Priesthood 2. Murder Mystery 3. E. B. McKee 4. Romance

© 2019 by E. B. McKee

ACKNOWLEDGMENTS

Thanks to the South County Writers Group whose critiques of the material were an ongoing support: Yvette Beau, Enid Flaherty, Dave Fogg, Michael Grossman, Nora Hall, Camilla Lee, Jane McCarthy, Terry Schimmel, and Jeannie Serpa.

Thanks to Michael Grossman whose patience is exceeded only by his publishing know-how. Special thanks to my editor Betty Cotter whose advice and guidance have been invaluable.

DEDICATION

To the McKee Clan

Contents

THE GIRL FROM DONEGAL

PREFACE

For writers of a certain vintage the decision to write short stories is determined by an unyielding actuarial truth. The odds of writing and finishing a series of ten- to fifteen-page short stories is substantially better than a four-hundred-page tome. The difference between an effort requiring a few months and one requiring a few years is substantial – a fact that the writer with a twenty-five-year affiliation with AARP should carefully consider.

An option for the mature writer is to take the short story/novella format, create a small masterpiece and – if mind and fingers remain in reasonable synchrony – continue to add stories and perhaps pack the pick of the litter into an anthology. If something untoward should occur at least the author will have something to show for his efforts.

I have taken this approach. What follows is a mixed bag of stories collected over the past two years. The primary genre is fiction but nuggets of truth are sprinkled throughout.

Gene McKee, July 2019

1

THE CALLING

TONY AND JIM WERE FRIENDS by default, their acquaintance having begun and been fostered at the end of an otherwise empty bench, where, as members of the 1961 St. Raphael basketball team, they had spent most of their time. They were the reserve players on the eight-man squad, the other nonstarter unavailable because of a season-ending injury. Their occasional presence on the court was limited to "garbage time," when the outcome of the game had already been decided by either a commanding lead or a humiliating deficit. Tony was convinced that the coach had forgotten their names. "You! You're going in! Get ready!" was his usual callout when either was being inserted into the fray.

Their lack of playing time was related to their physical attributes – or lack thereof. Tony's cadaverous frame brushed six feet, which was a couple of inches shy of the preferred height for his assigned position as the center. In spite of his painful stretching routines, Jim's recent growth spurt had faltered at five feet ten inches, which relegated him to the guard position. Moreover, his large butt and thick, muscular thighs didn't allow for the whippet quickness of the starting duo – both African-Americans. Jim's forte was the long-range, two-handed set shot, which he delivered with reasonable accuracy; unfortunately, it didn't fit the up-tempo offense the coach favored. Both seniors, their athletic careers were ending where they had begun – on the bench. For Jim, this was very disheartening, as he had worked hard to improve his basketball skills. Tony didn't seem to care. The two positive aspects of the seating arrangement: they had become good friends and had been rewarded with a bird's-eye view of the cheerleaders doing their splits, erecting their pyramids, and shaking their pom-poms.

Tony was from Bogotá, Colombia. His family had arrived in the United States three years earlier. His father, a physician, had accepted a pathology position at a local hospital. His mother, a nurse, had left the profession at the time of Tony's birth seventeen years earlier. Tony's younger sister was a student at St. Xavier's Academy, a Catholic girls' school in Providence.

Tony's father had completed his specialty training in the US in 1955, after which he had returned home and worked simultaneously at three hospitals in Bogotá. Tony's paternal grandfather had also been a physician – a surgeon of some renown – and the family assumed that Tony would follow in their footsteps. It mattered little that he had no interest in the profession. Then again, it seemed Tony had little interest in anything. Languid indifference characterized most of his activities: He moved at a slow pace, said little in class, and in conversation, his dark eyes often took on a dreamlike, vacant stare as though his mind had settled in a different place. On one occasion, he walked to the locker room at the end of the third period of a basketball game, thinking the contest was over; this hardly endeared him to the coach. Academically, he did well, his name appearing frequently on the honor roll. "Good thing," he told Jim, or "my father would make my life miserable."

Tony's father ruled the roost, making all major decisions in the family. Tony remembered his mother valiantly trying to change her husband's mind regarding issues that concerned the children. "But she always ended up crying. After a while, she just gave up." When the doctor decided that at age ten, Tony should learn to swim, he took him to the dock at a nearby lake and pushed him into the water. "I was scared to death. Screamed for him to pull me back up. He called me a sissy." Rather than backing off Tony was brought back to the lake for five consecutive days. Finally, he met his father's requirement, and the ordeal was over. The result: Tony was left with a wracking fear of water, an element he never went near again.

Jim came from lesser circumstances: The O'Briens, a family of four, lived in a basement apartment in a three-story walk-up in a tough part of town. Jim's father ran a car repair shop, his mother took in washing for a dozen or so local families and was an occasional substitute at the local grammar school. Jim's tuition was partially subsidized by the local Catholic church. When his older brother, Jeb, decided to work with his father and forgo college, the extra money improved Jim's chances of continuing school. His grades were good and, much like his basketball skills, were more attributable to persistence and hard work than to natural ability. His soft, freckled facial features, smiling blue eyes, and easygoing manner disguised a fiery disposition. Street-smart and tough, he was ready and quite capable of taking on anyone who disparaged him, his family, or his Irish heritage.

As Jim explained to Tony, "I live in a wop neighborhood, and if you don't tag one of them once in a while, they will piss all over you. My old man taught me from his own experience. He told me that when he started his car repair business, the grease balls came around looking for money. For his protection, they told him. He said okay and arranged to meet them in a week. He made some phone calls. When the tough guys came back, they were met by three of the biggest, most vicious bastards who ever came out of Cork City. Since then – about twenty years now – he hasn't been bothered."

"So, has your Dad mellowed out over the years?"

"Hell no! When I said your name was Tony, right away, he got suspicious you were one of them."

Frequently, during his junior and senior years, Jim went home with Tony after school to do homework. As they were both in the same homeroom and enrolled in the same college preparatory program, they had the same assignments. Once homework was finished, they played pool on a full-sized table in the basement family room. Tony's mother was a large lady who dressed smartly – usually in a white blouse and a flamboyantly colored skirt that brushed the floor – her full unlined face enhanced by firetruck-red lipstick and mascara-lined eyes. She brought them homemade cookies and soft drinks.

Tony's father was seldom there, as he worked at the hospital well into the evening. If he were to arrive, Tony would become visibly tense, knowing that his father would want to check his homework and would invariably make some negative comment. Occasionally, his dad joined in the pool game after taking off his jacket and loosening his tie. An excellent player, he was helpful with his advice, offering positive comments on the teens' play and presenting a side of his personality that was new to Jim.

One evening, Jim mentioned in passing that his dad was feeling poorly and had been coughing for a couple of weeks. The doctor asked an additional question or two and then dropped the subject. The following night when Jim's father came home from work, he reported that Tony's father, whom he had never met, had come by to see him. He said he listened to his lungs and gave him medicine from his bag. He also refused payment for his kindness, even turning down a fuel fill-up. "My old man was astounded," Jim said. "He couldn't believe his kindness."

Soon after the Easter holidays, Jim and Tony received their college acceptance letters. Tony was admitted to Tufts and Jim to Iona, a choice prompted by the promise of financial aid. Tony's father chose Tufts for his son because of its excellent premedical program and the recommendation of colleagues on the faculty. Weeks later, at a ceremony in the St. Raphael gymnasium, Tony and Jim, along with forty-five classmates, received their diplomas from the Bishop of Providence.

Before going their separate ways for the summer, Tony and Jim had a last night out. They went to see the movie *All the King's Men,* followed by sundaes at an ice-cream shop and then pool at Tony's house. Tony had been out of sorts all evening. Jim thought that it might be related to their friendship. Over the years, a healthy affection had developed between them, and the evening signaled a parting of the ways. Midway through their second game, Tony became quiet; he was obviously distracted, his lack of interest reflected in his poor play. He abruptly put his cue stick on the table and walked away.

"What's up with you?"

"It's just my old man, as usual . . . what he has planned for me when we go to Colombia."

Jim knew that each summer, Tony's family returned to Colombia for two weeks to visit relatives and friends. "What's that?"

Jim sat on the couch as Tony, hands in his pockets, walked around the room considering his reply. He then stopped and joined Jim. "Just between the two of us, right?" Jim nodded. "Okay. Here's the deal. The other night, he took me into his study and closed the door. Said he wanted to talk to me privately. Right away, I wondered what'n hell I had done wrong. He asked me a couple of dumb questions about school and then told me to take a seat. 'Tony,' he said to me, 'now that you're eighteen years old, you're no longer a child. You are now officially a man. And, there's a tradition for Spanish men at this time in their lives.' 'What?' I asked him. I thought he was going to tell me I had to get circumcised or something. He didn't say anything . . . like he was building up the suspense. He took a cigar from the humidor on his desk, smelled it, clipped it, and lit it. A big production. After a few puffs, he sat back in his chair. 'Tony,' he told me, 'the time has come for you to lose your virginity. Time to go to bed with a woman.' He told me that his father had the same conversation with him when he was my age. He said that when we got to Bogotá this summer, he was going to arrange a woman for me. I was stunned. Finally, I said to him, 'Aren't you supposed to at least like the woman you go to bed with?' He said that wasn't important now . . . that would come later. Now, it's more a rite of passage. And, most important, he told me, the pleasure will prevent any tendency to like men. He mentioned something about hormones getting all mixed up and going in different directions at my age. He said that's how the tradition started – to prevent men from having sex with men. I told him I wanted to find my own girlfriend. He waved his cigar at me and told me not to worry; he would take care of everything."

Jim listened, eyes wide, jaw slack. "Holy shit! Are you going to do it?"

"What choice do I have?"

Jim, a broad grin puffing his cheeks, put his arm around Tony's shoulders. "Buddy," he said, "I know a lot of guys who would kill to have a father like yours."

That was their last get-together. In the weeks prior to the family trip to Bogotá, Tony worked as an orderly at a Providence hospital. As he did most summers, Jim stayed with his maternal grandparents at their home in Tiverton. This allowed him to caddy at a local golf course, and the money earned was kept for personal expenses at college. The summer passed quickly. On a brisk early-autumn morning, Jim boarded a train in Providence bound for New York.

Iona turned out to be an excellent choice for Jim not just academically. He also found a sport at which he was naturally adept. At the tryouts for the college basketball team, he was totally intimidated by the wealth of talent. A housemate suggested that he accompany him to his water polo practice. He said that they were a great bunch of guys, animals both in and out of the water, and serious partiers. Jim discovered that he was made for the sport: a strong lower body, a pit bull tenacity, and a hearty reveler. Basketball became a memory.

In Jim's first letter to his friend, he asked how Tony had made out with his sex tutor in Bogotá. Tony wrote back that it had been, in a word, a "disaster." Details followed: Jacinta was attractive but was considerably older than Tony. Several attempts – assisted by hands, lips, and a bottle of wine – brought a spasm or two to his otherwise uncooperative jigger, and that was it. Part of the difficulty, he felt, were the admonitions regarding sex that had been seared into his brain from his years with the brothers at St. Ray's. At one point, he said that he prayed for help but that it only made things worse. Jacinta wasn't upset and advised him not to worry; she said that this was not uncommon and assured him that when he was less nervous he would be fine. She promised not to mention the problem to his father; she'd tell him that everything had gone well and that Tony had been "quite the boy." Tony could imagine his father's reaction if he knew the truth. He'd probably insist that, like the swimming introduction, Tony keep at it until he got the job done. At the end of the letter, Tony added that all had been resolved. He had met a girl at his summer job. Jacinta, he said, would be proud.

In a later letter, Tony mentioned that his father had retired and returned to Colombia. All family connections to Rhode Island had been severed. An exchange of Christmas cards marked the end of their friendship – or so Jim assumed.

Jim's years at Iona, where he majored in business, were similar to his high school exploits in basketball: He was a solid striver who never made the first team academically. But socially, he was a star: His sense of humor and upbeat personality drew others to him. He had a series of brief encounters with lady classmates over the four years, but felt most comfortable with the guys. A perfect night for this rowdy Irishman was attending a sporting event – preferably one involving Iona – followed by celebration or commiseration at one of their half dozen favored watering holes. He was able to hold his beer and was a great joke teller. With his razor-sharp repartee, and awash in the boozy affection of the guys, Jim was in his element. He often thought of Tony at these times, wishing he were part of the group and that he could share it all with him.

After graduation, business degree in hand, Jim took an entry-level position with an advertising agency. As a result of his usual diligence, attrition, and an Iona alumnus in upper management, he rose through the ranks, and within three years had his own cubicle and a part-time secretary. He found that his personality and fertile Gaelic imagination were well suited to the advertising world, and a list of satisfied corporate clients caused his Rolodex to expand steadily. In spite of entreaties by various family members to "meet a nice girl," he maintained his independence. "Just waiting for the right one" was his standard reply. He stayed in touch with his high school class and as their ten- year anniversary approached, he wrote Tony, wondering if he would be attending. He did not receive a reply.

For the reunion the gymnasium walls were crowded with banners, as well as photographs of athletic teams and their outstanding players. The spectator stands had been pushed back and folded, clearing space for the twenty-five or so tables that were scattered about the gym. In one corner, a bar had been set up, and most of the conversations between the attendees were taking place around it. The program had begun with a welcome delivered by the current principal.

Jim finished a second beer and headed back to his table. At that moment, a tall, dark-haired, fashionably dressed man entered the gym.

After a few seconds, he realized that it was Tony. The change in his appearance was startling: the scrawny body had filled out, the mop of hair that had seldom known a comb was now abundant and fashionably styled, and the pimply face and shallow cheeks were now clear and tanned. By any measure, the years had treated Tony well. A comparison to Fernando Lamas, a popular movie actor at the time, would be apt.

Tony went to greet Jim. They hugged for a long minute, both obviously pleased to see each other. For the remainder of the cocktail hour, they circulated among the crowd, trying desperately, in most instances, to attach names to faces they had not seen in years. Having chatted – at least with the members of their own class who were present – they decided to forgo the hot dog-and-bean supper and go out for dinner. They soon settled on an Italian restaurant, and after a quick perusal of the menu, Tony ordered a bottle of red wine that was advertised as being from Peru.

Conversation flowed without the awkwardness one might expect after a long separation. Tony mentioned, without emotion, that his father had died some months ago from a heart attack, totally unexpected. "I don't know if the shock of me quitting pre-med did him in or not. But he was very disappointed with me right to the end. My sister marrying a Puerto Rican – a struggling artist – didn't go down well either. She had moved to New York and worked in fashion design. From what she tells me, they get along fine. My mother went back to Bogotá and lives with her sister. And me, I hooked up with an import-export group doing a lot of stuff in South America. Got the job because I could speak Spanish. It's okay. Making a lot of money. That's about it. And you, my friend ... what's been going on with you?"

Jim summarized his uneventful work history and the family goings-on: His dad was still in the auto repair business and was "still on the lookout for wops." He mentioned his mother's cancer scare and his brother being in the Marines. He also told him that he had gotten together with Dan, a finance guy at the company, and that they were going into business together. They figured that Jim's people skills and client base and Dan's accounting prowess would be a good combination. "We're about the same age, have no domestic responsibilities, and don't mind working hard. Hell, if we fail, we're both young enough to recover.

I've told him all about you, by the way . . . how tight we were in high school. You must meet him sometime."

A second bottle was ordered, and over dinner, Jim asked his handsome friend how his love life was working out. "The way you're looking these days, you must be knocking them off pretty good." Tony said he was unattached at the moment and, in a tone more factual than bragging, mentioned numerous relationships with ladies over the years. His major success, he said, was with women whom he met on his flights to South America. He laughed. "Must be something to do with wine potency and altitude. I was actually engaged for a few months to a woman I talked through a run of turbulence."

Jim smiled. "Good for you. All the ladies you want. That's more than I can say," he said before adding, "but then, I'm not really looking."

Tony took a long sip of his Merlot. "I've pretty much given up, too . . . probably for different reasons, though. My problem is I can't seem to make any of them last. I'm okay with the fun part – the sex and the bells and whistles – but after that, things start to go flat . . . champagne without the fizz. The thought of commitment scares me. It got so bad, Jim, that I went to a psychiatrist. He said I had an intimacy problem – afraid to enter relationships for fear of them failing. He blamed it on my old man and his expectations for me. The doc – an old guy – didn't have much to offer. Every pot has a cover to fit it, he told me. There's someone out there who's just right for you. I looked at the guy. *You kidding me? Fifty bucks, and that's the best you can do?* As I was leaving, he added jokingly, 'There's always prayer.' And, Jim, it was that throwaway line that got the ball rolling."

They were the last diners in the restaurant, and their waiter was beginning to pace a few yards away. The bar had closed. Jim nodded toward the waiter. "This guy is getting nervous."

"He'll be all right. We'll give him a little extra with the tip. Just wanted to finish off the story. You're the first person I've told."

Jim finished the last of the wine, leaned forward and set his elbows on the table. "Okay, my friend, you have me intrigued. What's going on?"

Leaning back in his chair, Tony continued, "A few months later, I was passing a church and thought about what the old doc had said. So, for the hell of it, I went in and sat in a pew. The place was empty. I started to pray . . . well, more like regular talking. Didn't call Jesus or God by name . . . just spoke toward the crucifix behind the altar. I rattled on about the void in my life, the constant vague discontent, and about how I knew something was missing but didn't know what. I said that I'd tried booze, women, and self-help books, and nothing had worked. I went on like this for a few minutes. Then, I just sat and listened to the silence. I really wasn't expecting anything to happen – like an angel appearing or some heavenly sign – but I felt better just offloading the stuff; it was like going to confession. So, I started doing it two or three times a week. Then, one day, looking for something to read in the apartment I was renting, I came across a paperback: *The Seven Storey Mountain*. Know it, Jim?"

"Oh, sure! Think I read some of it. Thomas Merton, right? The monk?"

Tony nodded. "When he spoke about his years growing up, it felt like I was reading about myself. The more I read the book, the more I realized this was something I wanted to try. I spoke to a priest I knew, and he suggested I contact the Priory, a Benedictine monastery over in Portsmouth, where he had gone for retreats. So, I did, and that's where I'm heading tomorrow. I'll be there for two months. It's basically to see if I can handle that life and if they can put up with me."

"My God, Tony! A monk! I can't believe it!" Jim laughed. "Wait until your father hears about this. Watch out for lightning. So, how long does the whole thing take?"

"A while. You go through various stages: postulant for a year, novice about the same, initial vows, and then final profession. About five years. Can leave anytime."

"And the vows?"

"Yeah . . . poverty, chastity, and obedience."

"You okay with that?"

"I'm going to find out." Tony grinned. "You never know. I might get a yen for those bells and whistles again."

"I'm going to miss you, buddy, even if you're not around very much."

"I know. You'll be in my prayers."

The sour face of the waiter brightened when he saw the very generous tip given by Tony, who also picked up the check. "It'll be a while before I get the chance again."

The following morning, Tony left for Portsmouth, and from that point on, he disappeared from Jim's life. Jim contacted the monastery a couple of times to arrange a get-together but found it was not allowed during the non-professed portion of the postulant program.

About four years later, Jim received a letter from Tony inviting him and a guest to a ceremony where he and three others would profess their final vows. In the letter, he mentioned that his mother had died and that his sister was in Europe. "You're invited because my family's not around. But don't take it personally." In reply, Jim said he would be there and mentioned that Dan, his business partner, would be coming with him although he was not Catholic.

The ceremony was simple, perhaps a dozen guests clustered in the front pews of the chapel. Two priests celebrated the Mass, assisted by three young men clad in white hooded robes. The celebratory meal in the cafeteria was sparse; the ingredients, including the venison, were all products of the monastery. A tour of the property had been arranged, but Jim declined, saying "This is probably the last time I get to talk with my old teammate. You go ahead, my Methodist friend. It might do you some good." With some hesitation and a bemused expression on his face, Dan joined the tour.

Tony found a table in a sitting room that overlooked a broad stretch of lawn, bounded by trees and interrupted by small gardens, some with white trellises. The sun had begun to set, mist had formed along the water's edge, and on the bay, two sailboats, spinnakers billowed taut, were making for port.

Jim regarded his old friend. The movie-star looks were gone; the full, tanned face that he admired at their last meeting was now lean and pale; and his once-stylish mane now a clump of hair that looked self-cut – more like that of the kid he remembered from high school. "So, no regrets, Tony? You won't be defecting anytime soon?"

He smiled. "Things may change, but right now, I'm at peace with myself. And it's been that way since I arrived. We run a private school: grades eight through twelve . . . all boys. I teach Spanish and American history, and I love interacting with the kids. The majority live on campus, so we live and work together. They are less like students and more like friends; some are so delightful that you hate to see them graduate. Otherwise, my life is solitary, but I honestly never feel alone. God is always with me . . . my companion for life. I used to worry about failing. Now, it's not even in my vocabulary." He paused. "It could also be argued that I'm a coward running away from the real world, hiding in the shadow of our Lord, where self-esteem and ambition are not requirements. But I don't think so."

"Might as well tell you, Tony. For a long time, I thought I might be that companion. I guess you knew that."

"Yes." He paused. "I did. And there were times when I was inclined. But like my other relationships, it would have ended in the garbage heap. And I didn't want that to happen." Tony chuckled. "Plus, I had already been spoken for. Just didn't know it at the time."

Jim nodded. "You got the call. Off the bench and into the game. Who would have believed it back then?"

"God works in mysterious ways, does He not? And tell me, have you and Dan become close? It appears you have."

"Yes, we're doing well. It's been a couple of years."

"That's good. You'll both be in my prayers."

The conversation turned to reminiscences of high school, their basketball days, Tony's father, and the sexual tutor in Bogotá, all of which were remembered in hilarious fashion. Evening was approaching, the sun lowering in a blaze of color that flamed and flickered through the trees. The tour group returned, they went to meet Dan.

Goodbyes followed, with brief hugs and handshakes all around. No mention was made of meeting again, which lent an air of finality to the moment, the sense of a chapter closing and a new one beginning. Tony excused himself as he was expected to attend evening vespers. Dan and Jim watched as he, along with other cloaked figures exiting the cluster of solemn buildings, hurried in the direction of the chapel.

"Interesting guy, your friend."

"Yes, he is. I'm going to miss him."

"I hope not too much." Dan paused. "Just one question."

"Okay."

"Are we still all right? You know, after seeing the first love of your life again."

Jim smiled. "Better than ever. We have his approval and blessing, by the way."

"Good. In that case, let's find a cozy bar somewhere and have a drink."

"Sounds like a plan."

The sun had set, a cool mist sharpened the breeze. Hand in hand, they hurried to their car.

2

THE PLAN

D R. STEVE DEGNAN'S VISIT TO the nursing home presumed nothing out of the ordinary. Regulations required doctors to visit patients who received financial assistance from the state at least once a month. It was a treat to escape the office and the moderate bustle of town and enjoy the tree-crowded, lightly traveled route to the nursing home, especially on this brilliant Indian summer day.

Crestwood Acres, one of the oldest in the state, had been showing its age for some time – missing shutters, chipped white paint, a rash of broken, boarded windows – without any indication of repairs. Inside, the smell was pungent: a toxic brew of antiseptic, human excrement, and air freshener.

Accompanied by the chief nurse, Dr. Degnan visited his six patients, each assigned to rooms crowded with three others. Finding nothing untoward, he ordered routine lab tests, medications renewed, and progress notes updated. All very routine.

Finished with his last patient, Dr. Degnan prepared to leave her room when he heard a female voice say, "Hello, Steve."

He turned to a thin woman with stringy gray hair sitting in a wheelchair beside a bed. Nasal oxygen prongs were in place, and a cardiac monitor beeped at regular intervals. She gave a short wave.

"I'm sorry, I don't recognize you," Dr. Degnan said.

"Well, it's been a while." She smiled, her teeth discolored. "You look about the same. I've changed a bit. Take a guess anyway." Steve racked his brain, but the sallow, shrunken face before him offered no clues. *Probably some teacher I had*, he thought, *or a neighbor who knew me through my parents.*

Her deep-set eyes were expectant, but, after a moment, she said, "I'm almost embarrassed to tell you. I'm Jessica Abrams. We went to high school together."

Dr. Degnan was stunned. It couldn't be. The beautiful, blonde cheerleader, Junior Prom queen, and fantasy girl of every boy in the class? A flicker of unease came with the incredulity. "I never was good with names," Dr. Degnan stammered. "I recognize you now. How are you doing?"

Jessica explained that she had chronic lung disease. "The smoking did me in. The other thing, not being able to walk on my own," she nodded toward a walker in the corner of the room. "That part began the night I first met you at a party, thirty-two years ago this month. Do you remember that party, Steve?"

Dr. Degnan remembered it well.

Fairfield and Putnam High School had played each other in football on Thanksgiving Day for at least a decade. The skirmish provoked intense interest in both locales, as the winner had bragging rights as the best team in the county for at least a year. The epic struggle replaced the more mundane robbery, murder, and mayhem fare in the local newspapers. Torchlight parades and rallies ignited the citizenry. Members of the winning team were ensured part-time employment in local stores, free tickets at the movie house, extra scoops of ice cream at the drug store, and – most significantly – an improved standing with girls.

The winning quarterback was granted hero status. If it were the young man's good fortune to be blessed with good looks, then so, too, were the females who sought his favor.

In 1965, on Thanksgiving Day, the Putnam High School football team defeated Fairfield. To celebrate the victory, the Putnam quarterback, Ted Dillon, held a party at his house on the following Saturday night.

Ted's parents had approved the get-together and agreed not to return home before midnight. They also stipulated that alcohol was not allowed in the house. Neighbors were given fair warning. Invitations were extended to the team, cheerleaders, and coaches. The latter group promised to depart by nine p.m.

Though Steve and Ted were both seniors, their interactions were limited to the football field. Ted was the star of the team, a charismatic social animal, and the life of every party. Steve – a seldom-used, third-string halfback who kept to himself. On the gridiron, Ted played with athletic passion. Steve, if he played at all, was a passive presence. The downside of Ted's enthusiastic play was frequent unsportsmanlike conduct penalties, which were tolerated by the coach because of his athletic ability. Arguments with coaches and teammates made him an unpopular presence in the locker room. Perhaps the friendship of the two teammates flourished because they had adjoining lockers, and Steve was one of the few on the team who didn't think Ted a total pain in the ass.

The party began at seven p.m. Most of the students were brought by a family member. Many of the seniors had cars. As agreed, adults were out of the house by nine. By 9:20, one of the two kegs of beer that had been packed in ice had been removed from a car trunk and placed on the kitchen table. The house was a spacious colonial with a large living room and multiple smaller rooms where one could escape with a brew and a friend. The second floor was out of bounds, which was made clear by a rope strung across the banisters.

Ted, who had his pick of the cheerleaders, spent most of the night with Jessica – also known as Jess or Jessie – Abrams. They made an attractive couple. He was tall and darkly handsome with a taut, athletic build, she had the tanned, blue-eyed, perky look of a young Debbie Reynolds.

The party went well. The football players were especially animated as they reenacted the heroics of the big game. Prior to the party, all the glassware had been taken off the tables, and the framed pictures scattered throughout the house placed face down. Good thinking on someone's part.

By eleven, most of the younger kids had been picked up by their parents. Many of those who remained had paired off, getting a little together time in the dim side rooms. The music remained at a decreased volume. The dance area was empty. Ted and Jessie were nowhere in sight, so Steve assumed he had taken her somewhere more private.

Steve was putting a move on Nan, one of the remaining cheerleaders. Well into their second beer, they draped their arms along the fireplace mantel. Nan had allowed a couple of kisses, but Steve's enthusiasm hadn't been returned in either instance. As he leaned in for a third try, she shook her head and yawned. Never a good sign.

Ted suddenly appeared in the room, obviously distraught. He saw Steve and hurried to his side and whispered, "Steve, I've got a problem with Jessica." His voice squeaked with agitation. There were fresh cuts on his face.

"What's wrong with her?"

"I don't know. Come take a look."

Steve gave Nan a quick hug, said his goodbye, and followed Ted out of the house to a small bungalow on the back lawn. The lights were on. Ted opened the door, and they entered a large room. A bed was pushed against one wall. A counter and a small refrigerator filled a corner. Jessica lay sideways, her arms and legs splayed awkwardly on the wooden floor. Her eyes were closed and other than the occasional twitch of her lips there were no signs of movement.

"What happened?" Steve asked.

"We were fooling around on the bed. She fell off and bumped her head on the floor."

"It must have been a helluva bump. Let's get her back on the bed. Looks like she's breathing okay."

They lifted her onto a military-style cot. There was no bruising. She looked as she had earlier, even her bun was in place. A large lump was visible on the back of her head. The belt on her jeans was loose. Her blouse was unbuttoned.

"What am I going to do, Steve?" Ted's hands shook. He had a look of genuine panic on his face.

"Go get a bucket of ice. We can wrap her head in the ice and maybe get the swelling down a little. Then we'll decide what to do."

"Okay."

"And while you're at it, clear the place out. Tell them the party's over."

Steve cinched her belt and buttoned her blouse. Pinching her cheeks and shouting in her ears yielded no response. *May have to call the police,* he thought.

Ted returned. "Everyone's leaving. All the booze is back in the car. I told Jessica's friends to hang around. Said she was sick."

They positioned the back of Jessica's head on a mound of ice cubes, then lined the sides of her neck with the remainder.

"Okay, that's good. Now, Ted, I want to know what really happened."

"I told you. We were fooling around. She bumped her head."

"That's bullshit. She's been out like a light for ten minutes. She's got a swelling on her head as big as a baseball. Unless she wakes up real soon, we'll have to call the police. They're not going to believe you either."

Ted became quiet. Sweat glistened on his forehead. "Okay, we were making out on the bed. I told her I wanted a blow job. She said she wouldn't. I got pissed off. She tried to leave. I wouldn't let her. She clawed at my face, and that was it for me. I went ballistic and slammed her against the wall. She collapsed and fell to the floor." Ted paused. "That's what happened."

"Jesus, you could have killed her."

It was now eleven forty-five. Parents were due in fifteen minutes. Steve relieved himself in the small lavatory. When he returned, Ted sat on the edge of the cot, peering at Jessica. "I think something's happening, Steve. Take a look."

Sure enough, both eyelids fluttered. Encouraged by their shouts, her eyes slowly opened. Within a minute or two, she said a few unintelligible words and sat up. Her eyes had a far-off, vacant stare. She didn't seem to recognize them.

Her friends were called in. Holding Jessica up, they walked her around the bungalow for a few minutes and then to the waiting car. Just as they drove off, Ted's parents pulled into the driveway.

When they returned to school the following Monday, Ted worried that someone might report him to the principal, who would then call his parents and maybe the police. Add in the underage drinking, and who knew what shit he'd be in.

Steve noticed a change in his friend after the incident. Uncharacteristically quiet, the bluster and bombast that defined Ted, was seriously subdued – as though he realized how close he'd come to ruining his life.

But nothing came of it. Neither the school administration nor Jessica sought them out. It remained that way until February, when Steve and Jessica stood next to each other during the National Honor Society inductions. He wasn't surprised to see her there. A whiz in math, Jessica was on track to be class valedictorian at their graduation in June. During their brief conversation, Jessica never referred to the party incident, and Steve made no attempt to refresh her memory.

By mid-May, most of the college hopefuls had received their letters of acceptance or rejection. Ted had been accepted to Trinity College outside Hartford (his father was an alumnus), and Steve had gotten into the pre-med program at Stonehill College in North Easton, Massachusetts.

Graduation took place in June. At the start of the ceremony, the principal, Mr. Wilson, announced that the valedictorian, Jessica Abrams, was unable to attend because of a recent illness. He added that she had been accepted to MIT.

A few days later, Steve called Ted and suggested he contact Jessica, see how she's doing, wish her well. Ted declined. "I'd rather let sleeping dogs lie. I've been lucky so far. Let's leave it alone."

After that, Steve and Ted lost contact until Ted was introduced as a new member of the Hospital Board of Trustees at a monthly medical staff meeting fifteen years later. Neither had seen nor heard from Jessica. Not until she spied Dr. Steve Degnan at the nursing home.

"Of course, I remember the party, Jessica. I've often wondered what happened to you."

"Before we start, Steve, so we don't get interrupted, let's wait a few minutes."

Lunch was being served. A large cart with multiple drawers, pushed by a male aide, was at the door. Jessica's three roommates awakened as trays were placed on their bed tables.

"Are you going back to bed, Jess, or will you have your lunch later?" the aide asked.

Jessica lifted the cover from her meal: meat loaf, thick, brown gravy, green beans, and a scoop of mashed potatoes. Jessica tasted the potato with a finger. "Ugh, cold. I'll have it later after a warm-up. I'll just sip the coffee."

The aide nodded and left.

Jessica pushed herself up, adjusting the pillow against the back of the wheelchair. "Okay, Steve, we have to catch up. You first. What have you been up to all these years? Always wondered about you and Ted."

"Nothing too exciting for me. College, medical school, residency, three years in the military. All told, about fifteen years before I started my own practice."

"Things going well?"

"Yes, able to pay the bills, two great kids. Same wife I started with. Pretty boring stuff. But you, Jessica. You're the one I've wanted to hear about."

"I'm sure." She smiled. "You were there the night it all went down."

Steve nodded.

"Well, after I left school, I was confused and hurting. For a long time, I had no idea what had happened that night. I remembered going to the party and waking up the next morning feeling sick, but nothing in between. The only two people who did know were you and Ted, and you guys weren't talking. Everyone thought I had too much to drink. It took about a year before my memory was totally back. By that time, everyone had gone their separate ways. Probably just as well; I would have raised hell about what Ted did to me."

"Did you stay in Putnam?"

"No, I was in no shape to work, and my mom was by herself. My dad wasn't around. She had to go where the jobs were, so we moved a lot. We survived but barely. The big thing, what really did me in, were the headaches–and the dizziness and vomiting that went with them. They went on for years. It was horrible. I truly wanted to die."

"My God, Jess. Sounds awful. So, did you see anyone about them?"

"Yeah, the ER docs until they were sick of me. They took x-rays of my head. No CT scans back then. All negative."

"You must have had a blood clot," Steve said.

"Yeah, that's what they said. They called it a medium-sized stroke. They told me the headaches would go away when the clot eventually dissolved, and they gradually did over four or five years, but the weakness in my arm and leg was there to stay." She smiled. "Here's a tip for you, Doctor Degnan. None of the pills helped the headaches. Know what did?"

"No."

"Pot. One of the docs in the ER got the idea, and he supplied me. Must have smoked a ton of it. Saved my sanity but ruined my lungs."

"Excuse me," a voice interrupted. The aide had returned to collect the lunch trays. "I'll warm yours up later for you, Jess. Just give me a call."

"I will, Billy, thanks." Jess leaned forward and adjusted the pillow at her back.

"Anyway, Steve, things did get better for a while. I got a job that didn't involve much thinking or lifting, which allowed me to help my mom out a bit. I was even married for a couple of years, but the poor guy couldn't handle the situation and took off. Can't blame him."

"Any kids?"

"No, thank God. But, if you were to ask me what bothered me the most over the years, putting aside the physical stuff, my biggest disappointment was missing graduation. To be the valedictorian was my goal for four years. I worked my butt off to get it. My mom would have been so proud. It really was for her. She had so little to be proud of."

"Well, if it makes you feel any better, the principal mentioned you were going to MIT."

"I wish. Even that went by the board. My thinking had really slowed down, like my brain was in slow motion. I couldn't handle a place like MIT, so I called them and canceled."

Steve was impressed by how focused Jessica had become during their conversation. When she spoke about her misfortunes, her tone was not self-pitying but rather matter of fact. There was determination in the set of her jaw; a strong voice belied her wizened appearance. She was down but certainly not out. Steve knew clinically that anyone as physically compromised as Jessica, who couldn't breathe or walk without assistance, would have a difficult time turning things around, especially in a facility that offered so few services. He was certain Jessica knew that too. Her eyes, locked on his like lasers, had the desperate look of a prisoner searching for a way to escape.

They said their goodbyes and, in passing, she asked about Ted. "I heard he did pretty well for himself. Do you still keep in touch?"

Steve nodded. "About three to four times a year, we get together and yes, Ted has done well."

"What's he doing?"

"Well, his dad was one of the top dogs at Pfizer, a big drug company in New London. He was able to land Ted a spot in management. Timing is everything. Ted arrived there about the time Viagra was set to go on the market. He was given a heads up and bought as much stock as he could, even borrowed on his home. Then, my buddy Ted, who never clued me in, sat back and rode the Viagra rocket. He was soon a wealthy man."

"How wealthy? Like a millionaire?"

"He never told me exactly. But I think a millionaire a few times over would be a pretty good guess."

Jessica grinned. "One would do me fine."

Thinking about it later, Jess felt their meeting had gone well. She had known for some time that Steve was one of the visiting physicians at the facility. After many requests, she'd finally arranged a transfer to a room where he had a patient. Only had to wait for him to show up. She was relieved to learn he and Ted had remained friends and were in occasional contact and was confident Steve would tell him about their meeting. That was her plan.

The country club's fairways spread before them like plush green carpet. A series of homes – mansions, really – with a variety of architecture, including swimming pools, sprawled along the tree line. Three grass tennis courts were occupied by a group of ladies clad in white. A well-tended garden ran the length of the clubhouse porch where Steve and Ted sat, a hint of lilac and rose sweetening the breeze.

The suggestion for the get-together originated with Steve. He was attending lectures at the Yale-New Haven Hospital. Ted was delighted and suggested lunch at Woodlawn Pines, where he had been a golf member for many years.

Since their last get-together, neither of their appearances had changed dramatically, although Steve might have thought otherwise. The few strands of hair he had nourished with a variety of lotions for many years had departed, and he had also acquired a considerable gut. Ted's six-foot frame had lost little of its athletic cut from high school. The only clue to his senior status was the gray that had infiltrated his abundant thatch and an untidy stubble, which shadowed his now craggy features.

After some perfunctory small talk – Ted was recently divorced, and Steve had a son in medical school – and a quick review of the menu, Steve casually mentioned he had bumped into Jessica Abrams. Over the years, her name had seldom been brought up in their conversations for two reasons: neither had seen her since high school, so there was little to discuss, and it was a subject Ted had been keen to avoid.

"I bumped into her at a nursing home a few weeks ago," Steve said. "I thought you might be interested."

Ted took a long drink of his wine. "So, how's she doing?"

"Let's just say I didn't recognize her right off. She had a stroke and looks like hell."

"How's the nursing home? Any good?"

"Basic stuff. You get fed and have a place to sleep. Most of the patients are on medical assistance like she is. Other than bingo three times a week and a priest who says Mass on Wednesdays, there's not much going on. The place is way overcrowded. The staff does the best they can."

A waitress came by to take their order.

"Any suggestions, Ted?"

"Lobster roll. Can't go wrong."

With the order taken, Steve steered the conversation back to Jessica. "So, she's not in a very good situation is what I'm saying."

"Move her someplace else." There was a tone of dismissal in Ted's voice.

"For that, you need money," Steve said. "Look, the reason I'm telling you all this is because I think she's retrievable. There are some breathing issues, but the pulmonary guys do great stuff these days. Same with PT. It will take time, but I bet they could get her walking again. She says she's slowed down mentally, but I don't see it. Bottom line, Ted – we should help her. I can help with the medical stuff, but she needs more than I can give."

Their lobster salad arrived. Each ordered another glass of wine. "So, what do you expect me to do?"

Steve shrugged his shoulders. "You don't have to do anything. All I know is what you did to Jessica that night screwed up her life. A beautiful, brilliant woman stuck in a stinking nursing home for the rest of her God-given days, while you enjoy the good life." He paused. "Shit, Ted, she's our age. It just isn't fair."

"A lot of things in life aren't fair. Look, Steve, I don't want to get that pot boiling again. Soon as she and some shyster lawyer find out I got some money they'll be on me like bees on honey. I don't need that crap."

"She's not going to sue you. The statute of limitations would cover that."

"Bullshit, they'd sue a corpse for a few bucks."

Steve shook his head. "OK, Ted, my last shot. I'm sure I'm wasting my time. But, how about conscience? Do you still have one of those?"

Ted said nothing. He sat quietly for a moment, his facial expression unchanged. Then he pushed aside the remains of his salad roll and leaned his forearms on the table. "Steve, all you've said is true. But you should also know that in my entire life, and I'm fifty years old, what I did that night is my biggest shame. A shame I've carried around all these years, which I cannot wish or drink away. I never knew what happened to Jessica after graduation. I didn't want to find out. I made myself believe her life was good. Now, you tell me otherwise, and of course it bothers me." Ted straightened up. "So yes, Steve, I do have a conscience. How about we leave it at that."

There was no further discussion of Jessica or the party incident, other than Ted asking for the name of her nursing home. They spoke of other things.

The nursing home's supervisor called Steve three weeks later to inform him that Jessica had been transferred to another facility in the New Haven area. "She wanted to be sure you knew."

Several months passed before Steve visited her. Pleasant View Estates was in a neighborhood of stately, older homes. After a security guard took his name and examined his auto license, Steve passed between a pair of wrought-iron gates and moss-covered pillars to a circular drive-way lined with linden trees. The main house, a large Victorian structure with a wrap-around porch, had an impressive expanse of green sward and manicured gardens. Unfortunately, a hideous two-story modern brick travesty with air conditioners poking out each window had been appended to the original structure.

A woman seated behind an oak counter in the main foyer directed Steve to a room on the second floor. Soft classical music accompanied him as he walked down a wide, carpeted corridor and passed a series of rooms and a workstation where a woman dressed in a starched, white uniform and wearing a nurse's cap – a rare sighting – was bent over a computer. Steve was struck by the quiet. It was certainly a change from the hubbub and smells of Crestwood Acres.

The door to Jessica's room was ajar. A lady stood by a window reading a magazine.

"Excuse me, I'm looking for Jessica."

The woman looked at him. For a moment, Steve didn't recognize her. Then, it dawned on him. It *was* Jessica. Her appearance shocked him just like it had at the nursing home.

"Well, you found her."

"My God, Jessie, you look absolutely wonderful." And, indeed, she did. Her hair had been styled and colored a soft blonde with gray high-lights. Her drawn face and sunken cheeks had been smoothed and filled out, her opaque, shadowed eyes were now bright and mischievous. Her figure was back, albeit a softer, more voluptuous version – less the body of a cheerleader, more one built for pleasure. She took a few steps toward him without the aid of a walker and greeted him with a firm handshake and hug.

They settled into two easy chairs by a picture window that overlooked the broad lawn. A group of older men were playing bocce.

"So, tell me, Jess, are things going as well as they seem to be?" Steve asked. "I've never seen you looking so well or a nursing home as grand as this one."

"Steve, I don't know where to begin. It's so marvelous. The food, the staff, the activities. Physiotherapy three times a week. They're convinced they can get me walking on my own. A specialist has seen me for my breathing. I'm on new meds that have helped considerably. I only use oxygen at night now. An oral surgeon worked on my teeth, and – listen to this, Steve – I have my own dietitian!

"I'm delighted. And he will be too."

"I'm almost afraid to ask who's responsible for all this, like it's some kind of mistake no one's noticed yet. Medical assistance doesn't pay for this kind of care. That I do know. You said, 'He' will be pleased, Steve. Who is 'he?'"

"Who do you think?"

"Ted, but I want to be sure."

"Yes, you're right. I told him about you. We talked. He said he's never gotten over what he did to you, and I believe him. This is his way of making amends. I think now he's actually delighted to do it, a way to relieve some of the guilt."

"You know, Ted, I've thought about that night a lot." She paused. "But I was stupid too. What did I think was going to happen when I went into that room? I was so naïve. I should have known better. For a long time I blamed myself. But no more. I've paid my dues. Now it's his turn."

"So, forgiveness is not on your agenda?"

She turned, her gaze direct and cold. "I haven't forgiven, nor have I forgotten. Nor will I ever. But right now, he's part of my plan. I need him."

Their conversation wound down with the arrival of Jessica's roommate, a feisty seventy-five-year-old with red hair. Steve promised to keep in touch, and Jessica asked for Ted's phone number. "I should at least thank him for what he's done for me."

Three months later, Steve called Jessica, just to check in. As upbeat as the last visit, she told him about her progress: she was walking without a crutch, and her dental work was complete. She'd moved to the home's assisted living section, and she was taking courses online. "I'm hoping to get a teaching certificate and teach math at the grammar school level. I'm still not thinking as quick as I used to be, but with that age group, I should be all right."

"Have you seen Ted?"

"Yes, a few times. It was awkward to begin with, but we get along fine now. He takes me out for rides. We've had some good talks. He wants to take me to the Cape some weekend."

"Wow, you've come a long way, Jess. Whatever happened to the woman who would never forgive or forget?"

"Still here. Nothing has changed. What I planned to have happen has happened, beyond anything I could have imagined. And I don't want to blow it now. I'm at the threshold of being able to take care of myself. When I don't need Ted any longer, I'll say goodbye. He served his purpose."

"So, the trick now is to keep everything going as it is until then."

"Exactly. Another month I figure. Whatever it takes to keep him interested in me, I'm okay with."

"Otherwise, no feelings for the guy?"

Jess hesitated, "I'll only say it's sometimes hard to dislike the person who has given you back your life. But it's even harder to like the one who took it away in the first place."

"He may make you an offer too good to turn down."

There was the hint of a smile in her reply. "If he does, Ted, I'll definitely let you know. But right now, I've got to go. My hair lady just arrived."

"Bye, Jess. Good luck."

The phone clicked off.

Dr. Degnan never heard from Jessica Abrams again.

3

Bootleggers and Black Point

THE NORTHERN REACH OF SCARBOROUGH State Beach – an unencumbered stretch of sand located in Narragansett, Rhode Island – terminates in a cluster of sandy hummocks and a rocky out-cropping called Black Point.

Set back from the shoreline in dense, encroaching brush are the crumbling remnants of a sizable structure, its fissured skeleton glazed with green moss and scribbles of graffiti. This, the gatehouse, is the sur-viving remnant of Windswept, an estate constructed in the late 1800s. The main house occupied the stubby promontory of land that projects into the bay. Photographs of the time reveal an elegant home, its demise the result of suspected arson.

At that juncture, spared the assault of wind and waves, a placid, crescent-shaped cove and sandy cul-de-sac had formed. Currently the province of fishermen, walkers, and courting couples, its location once served a more nefarious purpose.

As a young boy, I spent time at Sunset Farm on Point Judith Road as a "helper" to John Carpenter, who, along with his wife, Ann Belle, managed the spread. My family lived a short distance away; we obtained dairy products and vegetables from the farm, and over time, the families became friendly. One day, after speaking with my father, John invited me to accompany him once or twice a week as he went about his chores. They didn't have children and probably enjoyed having a kid around.

Each spring wagon trips – horse drawn – were made to Black Point to collect seaweed deposited after the storms of the previous winter. Two or three wagonloads were the usual haul, which John used as fertilizer for the spring planting.

Accompanying us on those trips was Sam, a Narragansett Indian who worked with Mr. Carpenter when heavy work was involved. Taller than John, with arms and shoulders thick with muscle, he never seemed to tire. A beaded braid fell to mid-back; a red bandanna encircled his head.

Sam lived in a tent at the salt pond end of Sunset Farm and had all his life. His parents and grandparents worked there with black people during the time when large farms in South County were called plantations. Living off the land – blueberries, blackberries, and grapes grew in abundance – he bartered clams, quahogs, and crabs for vegetables and meat. During the bitter days of winter, John provided a room in the barn for him.

One day at Black Point, helping to load seaweed into the wagon, I mentioned to John how heavy the surf was at the main beach and how calm it was where we were. He nodded in agreement. "The bootleggers thought so, too. That's why they used to run their stuff in here during Prohibition."

"What's Prohibition?" I asked.

John, a large man with a big chest and protruding belly, pushed back his cap and wiped the sweat from his forehead with the back of his hand. "Back in the twenties," he began, "a bunch of people – mostly cranky women and religious folk–decided that liquor was ruining the country, making people do things that weren't right by the Lord. So, they said everyone should stop drinking. Tried to get some politicians looking to get elected to pass a law. And damned if they didn't. Called it Prohibition."

"So, everyone stopped drinking?" I asked.

"Hell, no, people drank more than ever." He smiled. "Tastes better when you're breaking the law. Shipped in from Canada mostly and the

West Indies. Shady characters with big schooners smuggled the stuff. 'Bootleggers,' they called them."

Visions of one-eyed pirates with black beards and muskets stuck in their belt, like in the movies, flashed in my head.

"On the way back, talk to Sam. He used to work for them."

In 1920, the Eighteenth Amendment to the Constitution (which Rhode Island never ratified) became the law of the land. This essentially prohibited the manufacture and distribution of alcohol – notably, not its possession or consumption. Exceptions to this law included the use of spirits in religious ceremonies and for medical purposes: doctors were allowed to prescribe one pint of alcohol every ten days if medically indicated.

Within days of the Act's passage, a bootlegging industry was spawned: vast amounts of alcohol, controlled in most instances by organized crime, were smuggled into the country, transported to major cities and distributed nationally. The Eastern Seaboard was supplied by an armada of vessels. Rhode Island became a major player in the enterprise by virtue of its 400-mile coastline and its antipathy to federal regulation.

"Sure, I can tell you about the bootleggers," Sam replied, when I asked. "Made a lot of money working for them. A lot of locals did, even the cops. Met at Black Point right at the beach we were just at. Some nights, two or three ships anchored out there in plain sight. The rum line they called it."

"If it was against the law," I asked, "how come they weren't arrested?"

"Because they were outside U.S. waters," Sam explained, "Anything beyond three miles was international, couldn't be touched. Anyway, the power boats that brought the stuff in could outrun the agents easy. Had old airplane engines, some of them."

Of the rum runners who plied their trade on Narragansett Bay Billy McCoy was the most well-known. Notably, he didn't drink nor was he involved with the crime syndicates. He dealt only with quality products: Cutty Sark, Seagrams, Gordons - guaranteed free of diluents and adulterants, the "real McCoy." Wealthy clients were often invited aboard his commodious schooner to inspect and sample his wares. Mindful of the economic benefits of a well-turned ankle and an enticing décolletage he employed a bevy of fetching ladies to serve these gentlemen. Transactions of a more delicate nature, it was rumored, were conducted in either of the two nicely appointed cabins mid-ship.

"So, Sam, what was your job?" We were heading up a partially paved Clarke Road back to the farm. I was driving the rig, with John beside me, and Sam, in back, astride the seaweed.

"Me and the others waited at the shore for the power boats to get close. Then we waded in, carried the cases to land, loaded them on carts, and hauled them up the path we just come up. Trucks were waiting at the road."

"Sometimes parties were going on at Windswept at the same time, I heard," John broke in, laughing. "Ain't that right, Sam?"

"Yeah," Sam replied, "you could hear easy over the water: bits of talk, piano playing, people laughing, probably drinking our booze. Everyone knew what was going on. Hell, all they had to do was look out the window."

"No police around?"

John smiled. "They were taken care of. You see, no one in Rhode Island wanted Prohibition, from the governor on down. No one felt bad making a few dollars. Hell, booze kept the state going until not so long ago."

In post-revolutionary war days – until Samuel Slater and Moses Brown processed cotton at a mill in Pawtucket, Rhode Island initiating the Industrial Revolution – the state's economy was sustained in large measure by the sale of alcohol, primarily rum. Scores of distilleries – thirty - seven in Providence alone – were scattered throughout the state. A robust market developed – exceeding a million gallons annually – encompassing the northeastern section of the country.

When we reached Point Judith Road, John took the reins. I joined Sam on the load of seaweed.

"Then what happened, Sam, after you loaded up the trucks?"

"We went down Ocean Road, stopped at some of the mansions, and stacked the booze in the cellars, then went to the hotels in town. Narragansett was popular in those days. Ain't that right, John?"

"More than Newport," John agreed. "Big hotels: the Imperial, Rockingham, Carlton. The Neptune Inn was popular. Had gambling there."

The Neptune Inn – now the Ocean Rose – is still in business. Originally called Youghal Cottage and the home of R. James Sullivan, it was subsequently sold and reconfigured. During prohibition the speakeasy, gambling tables – and a small chapel – were on the second floor. The 3rd floor, originally the servants quarters, acquired the indeterminate title of function rooms, they could be rented.

"And," Sam added," a secret stairway. Went from the cellar to a bar on the second floor," Sam added.

I looked at him closely. "Is that really true?" Sam loved to tell stories. Sometimes he made things up. "Did you ever go into the cellar where the secret passage was?" My ten-year-old imagination pictured fat men with scarred faces and shifty eyes, guns slung over their shoulder, standing guard.

"Yeah, of course. That's where we dropped the stuff off."

"Did you see it, you know, the secret stairway?"

"No, but there was a man standing in front of a big door."

"Did he have a gun?"

"No. Didn't see a gun. All dressed up he was—suit, tie, soft hat. But," Sam added with a grin, "he looked like a man who knew how to use one."

Back at the farm we dumped the seaweed around the field, to be plowed under later. I couldn't wait to get home and tell everyone about the bootleggers and the hidden stairway.

Decades later, my curiosity regarding its existence persisted. I was tempted to ask the manager of the Ocean Rose – to allow a walk through his establishment. *But, I reasoned, why chance spoiling a good story with facts. Let it remain where it began – in the imagination of a ten-year-old.*

And so it has.

4

A Reunion Of Sorts

THE MAN LIES PEACEFULLY ON the bed. The woman gazes at him and smiles. For five years she has looked forward to this moment. Finally, to have this handsome man who affected her life like no other, dominated her thoughts beyond distraction, now lying naked before her – a fantasy fulfilled.

The evening begins – as many evenings do – with Seth at his local bar, enjoying a beer at the end of an uneventful day. There is no tug of intuition, no hint that there would be more on his menu tonight than the usual three beers and a burger. For unbeknownst to Seth a capricious fate has arranged a scenario that will present him with a choice which – depending on the option he chooses – could alter the course of his life.

The pub where Seth is having his drink is a dim, square space, with blackened ceiling beams, wainscoted walls, small, opaque windows, and a ponderous oak bar, its pie-crust border fashioned with wood of a lighter shade. The uneven, log-hewn floor is partially covered with a rug drained of color, its worn nap riddled with drink stains and cigarette burns. Straight-backed wooden benches and small tables on which drinks may be placed extend along the walls.

This establishment began as the meeting place for the folk of Essex, Virginia, a village founded in the late 1700s by a contingent of settlers from that region of England. Within a generation the town – sired by

King Cotton – was born, and for many years it prospered. For reasons never totally understood – conscience, some think – one of the wealthy planters built a college on surrounding acreage. His bequest included certain provisos: that it be a liberal arts institution, that Virginia students be given admission preference, and that "sporting teams" be part of the curriculum.

More than two hundred years later, Seth Macomber, a country boy from a hardscrabble farm in the southern part of the state, entered the college as a freshman. Tall, strong, and fleet of foot, he enjoyed – as reported by the *Essex Echo* – four "golden years" as the star quarterback on the football team. He was rewarded with All-Conference honors each year.

During Seth's time, and as long as the town elders can remember, this public house has been the favored watering hole for the college's student body, especially after athletic events. The crowd that convenes – pints of Guinness or Smithwicks firmly in hand – vigorously celebrate the victory or, if an untoward result, lament with equal passion the defeat. These gatherings also provide those whose athletic feats are of an earlier time an opportunity to recall, dissect, and embroider their days in the sun. Seth is rarely absent on such occasions.

Four years after graduation, this favored youth who found in the muck and brawl of the gridiron athletic success beyond expectation is mired in the past. Five years have passed since his last touchdown pass, the final whistle long ago sounded. But figuratively Seth has never taken off the uniform; in his mind, especially after a beer or two, it's still third down and six yards to go, game on the line, the crowd chanting his name. He's like a child who won't leave the circus when the performance ends, hoping the clowns return, that the show will start again.

"Ready for another, Seth?" the bartender asks. He wipes his hands on the stained white towel hanging from his belt, takes a drag from the cigarette balanced atop the cash register. "See you're flying solo tonight."

"Yeah, between girlfriends. Letting the batteries charge up a bit." A wink accompanies his smile. "You know what I mean."

"Afraid not," Al replies, laughing. "My memory's not that good."

"Yeah, I'll have another. "And, it looks like you got a gang on your hands tonight my friend." Seth nods toward the John Jameson embossed mirror on the wall behind the beer pumps. Its reflection includes not only Seth's broad countenance and Al's bald dome but about fifteen other men, some strung along the bar, others milling about the space in boisterous conversation. All are colorfully garbed, with tanned faces and, if not wearing caps, white foreheads. A golf group, Seth figures, and with words like *birdies*, *traps*, and *drives* speckling nearby conversations, his suspicion is confirmed.

"Yeah, reunion bunch from the college. Good group. They were here last night, reliving the good old days. Having a helluva time."

"Good for them, and why not?" Seth replies. He turns for a closer look, seeking, perhaps, a familiar face. In spite of their ruddy faces and jaunty behavior, they are clearly a middle-aged group: hair retreating, some in comb-over mode, belts looped and lost on the down slope of their bellies. *Probably their twenty-fifth,* Seth figures.

Half way through his Corona Seth feels a push on his back, not unexpected considering the crowded quarters. He pays no attention. Seconds later, an insistent tap.

He half turns to confront the source of the prods. A tall woman apologizes for the interruption but says she would like to get to the bar to order a drink.

Seth pushes back his stool to allow her space. As she squeezes past, her profile, partially obscured by a broad, floppy hat, seems familiar. She turns toward him and mouths a thank you. With that comes recognition.

"My God, Connie, is that you?" His surprise is genuine but quickly tempered. If it is Connie – and her nod indicates it is – Seth remembers the trauma of their last encounter.

He suggests a retreat from the scrum at the bar to an open space by the jukebox. She smiles and agrees. A record is suspended at an angle above the turntable; a yellowed sheet of paper taped to the curved glass front informs: out of order.

She opens her arms to him, and they hug. During the embrace Connie mentions how pleased she is to see him.

"And you've hardly changed," he replies, appraising her at arm's length. "Looking as fit as ever." The compliment, though appropriately polite, strays from the truth. The lean, athletic build, the blonde hair captured in a ponytail, are as remembered; the drawn, pale face, shallow cheeks, and thin, tightened lips are unflattering newcomers.

Seth remarks on the serendipity of their meeting. Connie nods without comment, not wishing to disabuse him of the notion. For she knows Seth – the jock, the perennial sophomore – can be found here most nights.

Although not one to over think a situation, Seth is curious why out of the blue Connie's back in town. Is she here to exact the revenge she threatened at their last meeting, or something more benign – visiting friends, perhaps? If they settle in for a chat, which he assumes they will, he'll learn the answer.

As the only woman in the room and presumably aware of the frequent glances in her direction Connie seems uncomfortable. She turns to Seth. "Join me for a drink," she asks, "but somewhere not so noisy." He agrees that their meeting deserves an improved setting.

The adjoining lounge offers a half-dozen tables. None are occupied. Connie chooses one at the rear of the room. A small candle centers each of the tables, their light reflecting off sports trophies spaced unevenly on wooden ledges jutting from the walls. One corner has been cleared, a piano occupies the space. There is a smell of stale beer. They order drinks – wine for Connie, beer for Seth. Their conversation, tentative to start, skirts between college recollections and recent weather patterns in the Northeast. By the time the drink order is repeated, their posture has become more careless, their smiles and banter less forced.

"What brings you back?" Seth asks casually.

"An issue that needs to be taken care of," she replies. "One of those hands-on deals that can't be done at a distance. You know how those things go." Her voice hints of a shared confidence. "Tonight was meant to be an early turn-in." She pauses. "Never thought I'd be bumping into someone from the old days. And you, of all people. How lucky." The flip compliment – or is it sarcasm – adds to his wariness. "So, tell me what you're up to these days," she asks.

"Nothing much. Officially, I'm going for a master's in education – taking my time at it. Figure a couple of years. Picking up some change coaching at a local high school. Unofficially, I'm looking to hook up with a pro football team but no luck so far. And you, Connie? Fill in some of the blanks."

She takes a long draught of wine. "Well, as you can imagine, a lot of water has flowed under the bridge since we last spoke." In a manner reminiscent of a job interview, she ticks off her significant chronology: pregnancy, dropped out of college, had a daughter, joined the military, back-to-back rotations in Iraq, hospitalization for post-traumatic stress, now on disability. "That's about it." She pauses. "My first time back since our last meeting. Do you remember that day, Seth?"

Seth tenses. *Here it comes,* he thinks. "Of course. You told me you were pregnant and I was the father. Who wouldn't remember that?"

Seth had never before – or since – seen anything to equal the venomous rage, the cold, unrestrained fury she unleashed that afternoon. Screaming, swearing, kicking, raking her nails over his face, fists flailing at his chest, pummeling him until she fell exhausted into a chair. Even then, her eyes – icy blue, withered with fury – never left his face, the same eyes that calmly gaze at him now. In even tones, without a hint of rancor, Connie reminds him how fiercely he denied responsibility for her situation.

Seth nods. "I remember. Some of the stuff I said was pretty bad. But how did I know you weren't with somebody else? Hell, I hardly knew your name at the time."

In fact, Seth never did learn her name until later. He only knew her as one of the half-dozen groupies who trailed him in those days. She saw him at a frat party that night and nervously introduced herself. Fragments of half-heard conversation informed him that she was a junior psychology major and ran track. Although withdrawn, embarrassingly shy, and plainly dressed – nothing tight, no skin – she was pretty, Seth judged. And, as is often the case with the quiet ones, she later proved more vigorous than most.

Seth brings another round of drinks from the bar. On the opposite side of the lounge, a table is filling up. Connie adjusts her chair, turning her back to them.

"I thought you believed me when I told you I didn't sleep around." She shrugs her shoulders. "Looking back now I can understand why you wouldn't. But at the time, all I knew was my life was ruined, and you were the reason."

The golfers are departing the bar, arms around shoulders, laughter louder as they pass the lounge. There are no sounds of cars starting. Probably staying at the Holiday Inn down the street. *Good decision,* Seth thinks, *always wise to walk after the nineteenth hole.*

Connie leans over the table, pushes aside the candle, clasps her hands in front of her, and fixes her eyes on his. "Seth, there's something I want you to know." She pauses. "I'm bringing these things up not to reopen old wounds. I'm over the vengeance bit. I truly am. For me, now, it's about getting better. The mental health people tell me to face up to my demons, confront them straight on, not deny them. And you, Seth, are my resident demon." She shakes her head and smiles. "You're like an account that needs to be closed. Or a bill that has to be paid. I have to finish you off somehow, wipe the blackboard clean. I need to get to where the psychologists call closure so I can get on with my life. And who better to help than the man himself? And meeting like this – I swear it must be destiny – having a drink, talking back to the day, calmly, civilized, is a beginning, a step in the right direction."

"But Connie, look at the reasons…"

"Reasons to hate you," she interjects. "So, what should I do, go over the list every day and spend the rest of my life strung out over you? I can't. I won't. Life is too short; Iraq taught me that. You probably don't think so now. But you will."

Seth watches her as one would a volcano, looking for clues: a trace of smoke, a tremor, a hint that things could go south in a hurry. All he sees are eyes brimming with tears, a face etched in sincerity; an emotionally scarred woman who has had some bad times, trying to get her life back. And turning to him for help. He realizes how out of line his suspicions were, how groundless his concerns.

"Tell me about your daughter, Connie, he asks, "can't imagine how it was being away from her for so long - you know the Iraq tours. A little girl needs her mother around. Do you have a picture?"

"No, but they tell me she's growing up fine. Four years old now. I haven't seen her for a while."

"How come?"

"The counselor thinks I should leave her with the foster family until I can cope better. I get upset at times, and I take it out on her. The shrink thinks it's a subconscious rejection, you know, me not wanting the kid in the first place."

"That's sad to hear, Connie. But in a way I can sort of relate."

"How so?"

"Well, I was an unexpected arrival in my house. An afterthought that came along eight years after the last of my brothers was born. And that's pretty much how my mother treated me. Like a package delivered to the wrong address. My old man – who caught hell from her, by the way – sure'n shit didn't want another kid to support. All my time as a youngster it seems I was trying to get people to pay attention to me. Then, thank God, football came along."

"And now?" Connie asks, her smile teasing.

His disarming grin falls into place. "Yeah, still the same, still looking for attention. But I do know what it feels like when you're a kid and no one seems to care."

"I'm sure. But as bad as I might sound, Seth, I think – no, I know – I could have been a good mother." There is a twinge of remorse, of what might have been, in her voice. She takes a sip from her drink. "The whole damn thing just started off wrong."

"What's her first name?"

"An aide in the nursery called her Ginger. That sort of stuck. Anyway, Seth" – her tone turns impatient – "let's not talk about that stuff any-more." A frown appears on her forehead. "She's my other problem. And I'll deal with it." Reaching across the table, she slides her palm beneath his hand. As her sleeve shortens, a green Velcro watchband and a long, white scar appear on the underside of her wrist. "I'm so glad to see you again, Seth. Just to talk like we have." She squeezes his hand. "Guess it's true, you never forget your first one." As she speaks, she recollects his less-than-memorable effort that night: a brisk, workman-like coupling performed – without preamble – on a hardwood floor; his satisfaction quickly achieved, hers some hours later at home. Her foot grazes his leg. "And," she adds, "one I've never really gotten over."

Seth nods. A satisfied smile begins to form but is modestly restrained. *Decision time,* he thinks. *Go for it, or forget it. She probably could do with a little wave of the wand. Perk her up. Put some color in those pale cheeks. Hell, it's the least I can do.* "Tell you what, Connie," he says, "why don't we finish up with a nightcap at my place? Still at the same address."

Connie says nothing for a moment. She finishes what's left of her wine and glances toward the other table. The occupants are immersed in conversation. She checks her watch, which appears to be military issue. "That's it, then." There is a tone of finality in her voice. "Ordinarily I'd refuse, but the night has been a reunion of sorts. So, why don't we say in an hour?"

He nods approval. Connie leaves through a side door.

The apartment's dreary décor, Connie notices, has scarcely changed since her last visit. The TV is now a flat-screen model, and a shaggy rug in front of the fireplace – where they had lain that night – has been replaced with carpet. She has never been in the bedroom, and now, in the soft light of the bedside lamp, she sees clothes heaped about an unmade bed. He beckons to her. "I'll be right there," she tells him. "Need something from my handbag."

The man appears comfortable, lying in a tangle of mismatched sheets, his head propped by a folded pillow. A smile seems about to widen; his eyes have a quizzical look. As the woman gazes at his striking looks – wide, boyishly blue eyes, a mass of auburn hair, buff body, red-stained hole in his forehead, muscular arms flung to the side, rivulets of blood drying on his cheek – she feels an almost climactic sense of relief.

She drapes a thin sheet around his waist, and out of habit, tidies the bed. She separates the silencer from the revolver and returns the two pieces to her handbag.

Account closed, she thinks to herself. *One down, one to go.* She washes her wine glass and places it back in the cupboard. With much care she wipes clean anything she may have touched. This accomplished, she opens the door with her handkerchief and without a backward glance fades into the darkness.

5

The Golf Lesson

DURING MY EARLY TEENS WHILE caddying at the Point Judith Country Club I decided to learn how to play the game of golf. My family's summer cottage was only a ten-minute walk to the club, near holes 14 through 16. Not only were they easily accessible but well removed from the scrutiny of clubhouse and maintenance personnel. Many early mornings, my half-dozen wooden shaft clubs in tow, I played this section of the course.

This operation required planning. Ed "Old Man" Coulter, the head greenskeeper, began his rounds about six o'clock. The first business of his day was sweeping the greens clean of dew with a long bamboo pole after which he repaired any ball indentations and changed the hole location from the previous day.

These tasks took about ten minutes for each green. The key to my successful trespass: Mr. Coulter always started his routine on the first hole and took the remainder in numerical order. This allowed me, flailing away on the other side of the course, a good sixty minutes of playing time. An added security: Mr. Coulter made his rounds in a gas-powered cart, its back-firing engine loudly announcing his location.

On Monday, Mr. Coulter's day off, his younger replacement didn't begin his rounds until 7:00 a.m., allowing me time to squeeze in some holes on the front nine.

It was on such a mid-August morning walking down the fifth fairway that I saw someone sitting on the bench behind the 6th tee. Swirls of fog still masked the low-lying vegetation and, with a pale sun just clearing the horizon, identification was difficult. It appeared to be a woman wearing a white dress. That she was a member of the Country Club was my first thought. I considered turning around and beating it home but I had hit two decent shots, and with a chance at achieving par I decided it was worth the risk.

Finishing the hole – missing the par putt – I approached the tee. Indeed, it was a young woman curled up on the bench, her legs tucked beneath her. She wore a loose-fitting white dress. One strap had fallen from a shoulder.

She turned to me. "Pretty nice swing, young man. How old are you?"

"I turned fifteen a few months ago. More like fifteen and a half now."

She smiled, her teeth white and even. "That's a great age to learn this game." She sat up, adjusted the wayward strap, and swung her legs onto the grass. We didn't exchange first names but for reasons which will become apparent, she soon acquired one.

Her face in profile had a bony sharpness, which seen full-on gained a softer tone. Shiny, dark hair, its edges curled in the heavy air, fell to her shoulders; some loose strands looped over a pale, lightly freckled face. Beneath her eyes were dark smudges of mascara. A pair of red shoes lay some distance away, as if they had been kicked off. In spite of her somewhat rumpled appearance she had the look of someone who, as my aunt would say, "came from society." I decided she was beautiful.

"Are you a member here? she asked.

"No, I'm a caddy. I'm not supposed to here at all. That's why I'm out so early."

She smiled – more a complicit grin – "Your secret is safe with me. I'm trespassing too." She explained she had been at a party, "Over there." She waved in the general direction of a line of mansions along that stretch of coast. "The thing went on all night. Probably still going. Seems I had a little too much champagne, and a man I thought a friend treated me badly. Nothing a young boy needs to hear about. Anyway, I just needed to be by myself. I saw this beautiful golf course, found a bench and had a good cry."

"Are you okay now?"

"Yes, much better, thank you."

At the time, I was going through my F. Scott Fitzgerald phase having read "The Great Gatsby" some months earlier. Listening to her story, her features bathed in the soft shades of morning, she easily became the Daisy of my imagination. The backdrop: an elegant mansion on the ocean, a party that lasted until dawn, jazz music, risqué dances, the jaded wealthy enjoying their careless pleasures – even the callous cad with the slick-backed hair who had driven her to tears – fit nicely my scenario.

"And, before I go I want to see your tee shot," Daisy said.

Confident and eager to impress, I set up for the drive. Brassie in hand I made my swing. The ball I expected to see far down the fairway had trickled into rough a few yards away. Embarrassed, I picked up my bag and began to head off.

"Where are you going? Get back here. Let's try it again." She stood up, her dress billowing around her. In spite of my distress, I was struck by how tall she was and how nicely the sun silhouetted her legs through the thin fabric of her dress.

I retrieved the ball.

"Okay," she said, "when I was your age I was given a tip. Very simple. Maybe it'll work for you. Shall we give it a shot?"

"I guess so," I mumbled

Daisy took the ball and teed it so high it was barely fixed in the ground. "And when you get ready to hit I don't want you to focus on the ball.

"So, what do I look at?"

"The tee. If you really, really concentrate on hitting it square your swing will naturally slow down. Let's try it."

I followed her instructions, and the ball was soon a distant speck bouncing down the center of the fairway. Daisy seemed as pleased as I was. "That, my friend, was a golf shot."

I thanked Daisy for the help. She said she was going to sit a while longer. She gave me a hug, and we said our goodbyes.

I floated down the sixth fairway. At the finish of the hole, I turned around for a final wave. She was gone.

In case you're wondering, Daisy's tip didn't turn me into a scratch golfer. Not even close. In its stead I have the memory of a luminous August morning, standing on the sixth tee at Point Judith Country Club. I had just hit the best drive of my entire life and was being hugged by a beautiful woman in a filmy white dress, the brush of her hair soft on my cheek – the stirrings of adolescence still remembered these decades later. F Scott would be pleased.

6

A Lady in Waiting

BETH, AN ELDERLY WOMAN, LIVES in a gray-shingled carriage house. Being of similar vintage, each could be described as
having weathered well. The view from the living room includes a sweep
of well-tended lawn that stretches to a squat hedge, beyond which, at
some distance, lies an expanse of ocean. A courtyard in front is framed
by two buildings, one of which once stabled horses, the other a storage
room for riding tack.

Clint, a heavyset, middle-aged man whose undistinguished face is
made more so by gray, rimless glasses, is a frequent visitor here. The
reason: the owner of the property and only resident is his aunt who,
with scant awareness, is approaching her hundredth birthday. Clint, as
her only surviving relative, has assumed responsibility for her care. He
accepts this position without hesitation. Beth – an amended Elizabeth
– was an imperious presence during his youth and formative years in
her role as surrogate mother. From the outset it was apparent she wished
to mold him into the son she never had – a project that never met her
expectations.

His visit this spring day is a routine one, a check-in with the nurse's
aide on duty as to any untoward events over the previous twenty-four
hours and an opportunity to spend time with his charge. Their conversations of late have been difficult; a shroud is closing around her once agile
mind. Periods of lucidity that could be measured in hours three months

earlier have been reduced to minutes. Long-ago events are sometimes captured, the occasional visitor is remembered – brief flares that pierce her darkness. Clint and Blanche, one of the aides – a black lady – are the only people who spark consistent recognition.

Beth looks up when Clint enters her room. She's sitting in a chair, legs elevated, loosely covered with a light blanket. He sits beside her and takes her hand. She smells of Gold Bond powder.

"Who are you?" she asks, squinting in his direction.

"Clark Gable. Who were you expecting?"

"*Gone with the Wind.* I remember you."

"Good girl, Beth. Right on the ball today."

"He was a nice man. Like you used to be."

Clint smiles. *Typical Beth,* he thinks, *Never a compliment without a sarcastic dig.*

During her considerable lifetime little has passed Beth by. Clint remembers as a youngster, his imagination being fired by her recollections of the exotic places she had visited: the Taj Mahal at dawn, moonlight streaking an inky Ganges, the poppy fields at Flanders. Though equally lofty, Curt's travel ambitions have, of necessity, been more confining.

Beth has loved and been loved in return. To what extent in either instance is difficult to ascertain. In spite of a series of male friends, marriage has eluded her, as it has her nephew. Her conversations identify a well-informed mind; a stack of books – mainly biography and history, rarely fiction – crowd her bedside table. Physical demonstrations of the hugging, kissing variety are not part of her social armamentarium. Maudlin, teary-eyed exhibitions are treated with similar disdain. In Clint's memory the word "love," as applied to another person, has never escaped her lips. Clint saw her cry only once: when his father, her brother, died.

He remembers her as a tough taskmaster during his childhood, especially in matters educational. Beth was a teacher. On his visits no conversation exceeded a sentence or two before his latest grades were requested. If, at report card time, a poor mark was revealed, Clint could be sure his next visit would include a test – devised by her – in that subject. Although he tried, Clint knew his grades consistently disappointed her, and she wasn't shy about informing him of her displeasure.

Over the years there have been two significant bumps in their relationship. The earliest involved employment, the other romance.

After a spotty high school career, Clint was not accepted at any of the four colleges to which he applied. He refused Beth's offer of tutoring and summer school as a means of improving grades so he might reapply. Standing up to Beth for the first and last time, he told her he wanted to attend a technical school and learn a trade. Beth's response was swift and predictable.

"It's either a proper college or nothing at all. If you want to be a mechanic or something like that, you'll do it on your own." Her voice scathed with derision.

"I'm not trying to hurt your feelings, Aunt Beth. But that's what I want to do." And that's what he did.

A series of low-paying occupations followed, none of which included adequate salary or the possibility of advancement. During her lucid years Beth regularly reminded him of his "stupid" decision. She needn't have bothered; his present situation as a custodian in an engineering company is a daily reminder.

The other squabble involved a woman. At the time, Clint was twenty-five years old and had never had a significant romantic relationship. The occasional bar conversation - fueled by gin and tonics – offered promise, but nothing extended beyond closing time. An ungainly appearance – rotund body, thinning blond hair, dough-like cheeks, a sag of flesh beneath his chin – offered little appeal to women.

Mary, a temporary secretary in the same company, a year older than Clint and similarly proportioned, saw past the externals and found a kind man with a quick intelligence, quaint courtesies (opening doors for ladies) and a quirky, self-deprecating brand of humor. They met at the company's Christmas party, and over the next few months remained friendly. Formal dates followed, during which mutual interests (reading and travel), responsibilities (home-bound, debilitated relative) and frustrations (job and weight) nurtured a budding chemistry. Their compatibility became such that within a year of their meeting, plans were made to become engaged.

Beth, unaware of the relationship, reacted to the news with shock, followed by a host of questions relating to Mary's job ("No money in that, not even full time"), marital history ("Not married at her age? Something wrong there"– never mind the irony of her statement), and ethnicity – ("Marry an Italian and you get the whole, stinking tribe along with her").

"But Aunt Beth, I really like her. First time ever I've felt this way. And you'll like her too, when you meet her. Has a great sense of humor, just like you."

"Humor doesn't pay the bills. And I don't want to see her. Look, Clint," she added, her tone less harsh, "neither one of you has a pot to piss in. What if kids come along? Then what happens?"

"We'll worry about that then."

Her smile was dismissive. "Typical Clint response," she retorted, "no thought of consequences. Just like the college decision." She paused. "Look, Clint, I'm not against you getting married. I'm just being practical. Wait a couple of years. When you're in a better situation. You're both still young."

Similar conversations with Beth, variations on the same refrain, continued for days. The option of waiting a while began to make sense to Clint. *If it's the real thing,* he thought, *it'll stand the test of time. If it doesn't, then we did the right thing by waiting. And we can still see each other in the meantime.* A hiatus, he decided, was the correct decision.

They met at a coffeehouse. Mary remained composed as he quietly explained the logic of deferring their engagement plans. "It just makes sense, Mary, me getting in a better place, saving up a little. We can still see each other." He failed to mention the overriding reason: not wishing to incur the wrath of his aunt.

Mary pushed her untouched coffee away and clasped her hands in front of her.

"Clint," she began, "I have never been so sure of anything as the two of us doing well together. I very much want to marry you and start a family. But if you wish to wait, I'll accept your decision. But while you're finding your better place, I won't see you, write you, or talk to you." Her cheeks were flushed, dark eyes flashing, her voice lowered. "And if, in the meantime, someone suitable comes along, I will hesitate perhaps a second before accepting his proposal. So that's my position. You know how to get in touch with me." She paused. "Now, please leave. I want to cry."

That was two years ago.

Though in good humor most of the time, Beth is not without days of despondency, times when she feels the Grim Reaper is about to cast his pale shadow.

"I think today's the day," she announces on such occasions. "Something tells me I won't be here tomorrow."

Bolstered by a reassuring nod from the aide signaling his aunt's status is unchanged, Clint offers his standard response. "So, today's the day, Beth?"

"Yes, I'm pretty sure this time."

In feigned exasperation, Clint responds, "Promises, promises, Aunt Beth, that's all I get from you. Yet here you are, still around. And looking pretty good by the way."

Because of hearing difficulties, sentences are often repeated but when the transmission is successful, her eyes brighten, a smile appears and a cackle or two approximates a laugh. A cup of tea puts any lingering concerns to rest.

Sunday is reserved, no matter the weather, for Beth's favorite activity: the Sunday afternoon car ride. Wheeled to Clint's pick-up truck, she is easily bundled into the wide passenger seat, a blanket tucked beneath her legs. Clint takes the same route each week, hoping she will gain a comfortable familiarity, but for Beth each drive is a new adventure. The conversations are virtually unchanged from week to week.

She loves to stop and gaze at the ocean. "Isn't it a beautiful color today? Is that a sailboat out there? Isn't it pretty." All echoes from the past.

Clint, watching her, wonders what it must be like to look at the world for perhaps the last time – the gulls that wheel above the ocean, the stretch of crowded beach – scenes perhaps never to be seen again.

The poignancy of the moment saddens him; the reality of it never enters her mind.

One stop seldom skipped is a small pond about twelve feet across, dense with lotus plants. The gaudy palette of saucer-size blossoms meld one to the other, a cauldron of color swaying in the breeze. Beth stares as though mesmerized, agreeing to push on only when promised they will still be there next week.

Then a change of scenery: a winding country road flanked by tall, maple trees, their branches forming a canopy overhead. Occasional bursts of sun escape as the truck passes underneath. Large farms and newly constructed homes stretch on either side. Common to each and the surrounding tracts of land are stone wall borders. Beth admires their walls, especially if well maintained and free of encroaching vines and vegetation. Something about their symmetry, the clean, strong, non-friv-olous look, appeals to her. Perhaps it recalls her childhood spent living on a farm similarly bound.

The excursion finishes with a cup of tea and a plain doughnut. On the way home she closes her eyes and rests.

The month after Beth celebrated her century of existence coincides with a slow but persistent decline in her condition. Gradually over several days her breathing, although regular, becomes more shallow. Fluids are maintained, her mouth kept moist. She appears comfortable, just a body wearing out, a heart that has beat for a hundred years calling it a day.

Medical intervention is not called for or needed; there is no indication of distress. The prognosis succinctly supplied by Blanche is "any day now."

A call is placed to the pastor of the local Catholic Church. Within the hour he has anointed her and offered prayers for the dying.

Her time comes on a warm midsummer Sunday afternoon. Blanche meets Clint out front as he arrives at the house.

"I was just about to call you," says Blanche.

In his aunt's bedroom, Clint brings his chair to the side of the bed and takes her cold hand, the knobby, arthritic fingers clenched and unmoving, the skin a thin parchment waxy to the touch. Scarcely per-ceptible breaths are occasionally interrupted by a short sigh.

"How long has she been like this?" he asks Blanche.

"'Bout a half-hour now. Had a pretty good day up to then."

Lusterless hair, combed straight back from her forehead, splays onto the pillow. Her eyes are closed, lips pursed, skin shrunk taut over high cheekbones and a strong, still determined jaw. She seems totally composed, as if in a waiting room, patiently waiting to be called.

Clint turns to Blanche. "Still has a beautiful face, even now."

"That she does. I have more wrinkles than she has, for sure."

When his attention returns to Beth, he finds she has turned her head on the pillow, and her eyes, suddenly bright and clear, are staring at him. There is the hint of a smile. Clint leans toward her.

"Beth, talk to me."

Her gaze fixes on him. Her lips begin to move. Then in the barest rustle of sound comes the whisper, "Thank you." In the same moment, as if a shade is being drawn, her eyes close. Then she sleeps, not to wake again.

Beth's request, repeated over the years, of not being waked is honored. The scarcely contained conviviality on such occasions she felt was disrespectful both to the family and the guest of honor. The Mass, which about fifty people attend, is as she instructed: a simple ceremony. Clint does voice his thanks to the attendees for their presence and expressions of sympathy.

At the cemetery a brisk breeze threatens the frail canopy over the gravesite where Beth is laid to rest. In his remarks the Father scans the exemplary life of the deceased. He concludes with a message of consolation: "A child of God has returned to her Maker. Always held in His heart, she now rests in His arms. And she will for all eternity."

Beth, although a devout Catholic, often wondered if death was the end of the story or if there would be another chapter. *Well,* Clint thinks, *she sure'n hell knows the answer now.* The only reward she ever wanted was to see her mother again.

As the symbolic shovel of dirt rattles off the metal casket, Clint's eyes begin to fill. Beth's dictum regarding such displays come to mind. He brushes aside the wayward tear, and the moment passes.

After a sparsely attended reception in the parish hall and his official duties completed, Clint feels he could do with a drink, something to ease his melancholy. But knowing, as the song says, "There's nothing sadder than a glass of wine alone," he decides to fire up his truck and retrace their Sunday excursion for the last time. *Hell,* he thinks, *nothing's changed.* The seat is still adjusted as she likes it, the Tetley tea bags she prefers stashed in the glove compartment, an oldies radio station tuned in – and Beth sitting beside him, only a memory away.

And she enjoys the day. As Clint describes the sun-baked beaches and the flotilla of sailboats racing off Newport, the vivid blossoms in the gardens they pass, the clean line of stone walls along a wonderfully shaded country road, he can see her smile and hear the delight in her voice. Heading home, he turns off the radio. As always, about now, her eyes close and she rests.

He pulls into the courtyard. The afternoon is fading, blue shadows are settling among the shrubs, the house and side buildings gray and bleak in the gloom, a distant surf the only sound. A sense of melancholy fills the space.

He pushes the seat back in the pick-up, extends his legs and lights a cigarette. His mind wanders through the day's events and the sprawl of his life with Beth. There is a mix of emotions: Sorrow at the loss of the most important person in his life, gratitude for the extraordinary investment of time and treasure she made on his behalf, regret at his lack of achievement – success being the credential necessary to gain her approval. There is the satisfaction of being able to give back during her last years, and relief at being loosed from the purgatory of unmet expectations. For these he is grateful.

Sometime later, driving home, it occurs to Clint that for the first time in memory he has the ability to live life as he wishes, no permissions required, no decisions up-ended, to succeed or not on his own – his last excuse now departed.

And if he wishes to seek out a woman he hasn't seen in two years, so be it.

7

A Night at the Theater

THE GENTLEMAN WHO SIGNALED he wished to speak with me wore a pleasant expression, but the conversation was brief and to the point. "I'm afraid you two will have to leave."

"How come?" I countered. "The tickets are paid for. We're not bothering anyone."

The year was 1955, and the conversation was occurring at the Theater by The Sea – a repertory company in Matunuck Rhode Island that offered stage productions each summer. I was twenty-one years old, as was Priscilla, the woman with me that evening. This was our first date – and as fate would have it – our last. The gentleman who addressed me was Harold Schiff, the manager of the theater.

"But you are bothering others," he responded and pointed to a series of empty seats in the area where Priscilla was sitting. Most had retreated to the side aisles. One woman covered her nose with a white handkerchief.

"Those customers," Schiff continued, "also bought tickets. Now the whole lot of them have threatened to leave. And they want their money back unless you and your girlfriend remove yourself."

The incident began shortly after we took our seats in the balcony. I had noticed a few stares from people in our immediate area but dismissed them, thinking perhaps they were admiring my date – tall, blond, tanned shoulders, and wearing an attractive summer frock. The houselights had dimmed, and the show, a musical, was about to begin when Harold – a tall man with black hair, wearing an ascot–made his appearance.

"So, what's the problem?" I asked.

I knew what the problem was. I had encountered it before, and I thought I had made adequate preparations: an extended time in the tub, a brutal soap that puckered my skin, and a head-to-toe dosing of Old Spice cologne. But obviously to no avail. The lack of air conditioning and the humidity of the night had tipped the scales.

Most jobs, if not all, have their occupational hazards: the dust in coal mines, the fatigue of the long-distance trucker, the precariousness of a high-wire artist on a windy day. Then there was my summer job and the smell associated with those who cut fish for a living, an aroma pungent enough to make eyes water and stomachs turn. A higher order of acridity – well beyond the sweat and skunk variety that's banished with a shower and scented soap – this essence burrows deep into the dermis and leaches out its noxious bouquet until the skin finally sloughs away, replaced with untainted cells.

In the dating arena, it was catastrophic: one good whiff and I was history. A bunch of us from the Fisherman's Co-Op in Galilee often went to Lake Mishnock in West Greenwich for dancing on Saturday night. The reasons were threefold. We went for the women, to enjoy the great country music provided by Eddie Zack's band, and – because the top half of the walls in the hall were screened – we could take advantage of the brisk breeze that billowed from the lake. If you could keep your partner upwind as you circled the floor, you had a fair chance of another dance or two. If she had a bad cold, you could be good for the night.

Priscilla was the exception. Her two older brothers – who had arranged our introduction – worked with me at the Co-Op. By living with them, exposed to their stench for many years, she had developed a tolerance.

"The problem is the smell you give off," Mr. Schiff said. "It's overpowering. It makes people nauseated. I feel a little sick just talking to you."

"I work with fish."

His eyes narrowed, the soothing voice now sullen." I don't care what you work with. You have to leave."

I glanced at Priscilla. The entire balcony – except for a few stalwarts in the back row–had emptied. Even her tan couldn't hide the flush of embarrassment. A slow clap had begun from those in the ground floor seats, upset with the delay of the show.

I went over to her. "He wants us to leave. He runs the place."

"Your smell?"

"Yeah."

"I thought so. Then let's go. We're holding everything up." She stood but remained bent at the waist, not glancing in any direction, hoping, it seemed, to avoid recognition.

I took her hand. "Okay, Mr. Schiff, we'll leave. I want my money back, though."

"You'll get your money back. I'll also give you tickets for an upcoming show for free." He hesitated, "If you get yourself fixed."

The clapping was becoming more insistent. Harold signaled to the band leader, and the overture began. We followed him down the stairs to the lobby where he refunded our money, but he modified his offer of free tickets. If I came back, I would have to present myself for his "evaluation" before being allowed admission.

We wished him a successful season and headed off.

The evening was clear, the moon was approaching full, banks of clouds were scudding past.

"While we're here, might as well have a beer." I nodded toward a nearby building, formerly a barn like the theater and now a lounge.

Priscilla thought it a good idea.

We followed a stone-strewn path bordered on each side by a trellis entwined with honeysuckle, the space between heavy with their fragrance. Suddenly we heard the scrunch of shoes on the gravel behind us. We turned. Harold Schiff was walking rapidly in our direction.

Panting from the exertion, he caught up with us. "Where are you two going now?"

"To the bar for a drink."

"You can't do that."

"Why?"

Harold's cravat had loosened during his exertion, carefully placed strands of hair were askew. He was irritated.

"For the same reason I took you out of the theater: you smell."

"But there won't be anyone in the place. Everyone's at the show." I pointed to a window in the barn that displayed a barman and a line of empty stools.

"No matter. I can't take the chance."

Priscilla pulled at my hand. "Please, let's get out of here."

Some small chatter followed, but soon we were in my pickup truck heading home, my carefully planned night in ruins. Priscilla dismissed suggestions of a walk on the beach or a drink at the Surf Bar in Narragansett without discussion. I put my arm around her shoulders and mentioned how sorry I was the night had gone as it had.

She shrugged my arm away. "It's okay. Don't worry about it."

At that moment our date effectively ended.

Two days later I called Priscilla with the thought of meeting again. She refused. I persisted. "It won't be that bad again. It can't get any worse."

"It's more than that. Remember when you put your arm around my shoulders?

"Yes."

"Well, there's a big rash there now. I'm seeing a doctor tomorrow. I think I'm allergic to your skin."

"That's really weird. I don't have any rashes."

"I never had any either, ever, until I made contact with you."

"I'm sorry. Call me when you get better."

She said she would.

Her condition apparently never improved; fifty- plus years have passed, and she has yet to get back to me!

Some years later, long after I severed my connection with the fish business, I had occasion to attend a production at the Theater by The Sea. Waiting in the lobby before the show, I turned and saw a man staring at me. Though heavier and hair grayer, there was no mistaking

Harold Schiff. He had a puzzled look on his face. Then came the flash of recognition.

He approached me. "It's you," he said. "You're back."

I acknowledged I was.

We remembered the night of our first meeting. He said that in all his years dealing with the public, that was one of his most memorable recollections. As his lips moved in the telling, so did his nostrils, flaring and contracting, discreetly sniffing, still suspicious after all these years.

The show was about to begin. Before we parted I asked him if I passed inspection.

He grinned and said I had.

"And the bar?"

Harold laughed, a loud guffaw. "Don't push it, fella. I'll let you know later."

8

THE GIRL FROM DONEGAL

The only customer in the public house that September evening was a young man, his long legs twined around one of the half-dozen stools that lined a curved oaken bar; a newspaper poked from his jacket pocket. His order of a pint of stout, now settling beneath one of the pumps, was attended to by a squat, ruddy-faced barman, a cigarette hanging from his lips. The pub, a worn, dismal space reeking of old porter and mold, offered little pretense of style. The dull afternoon sun slanted across four tightly placed tables, each centered by a wax-encrusted, empty candle holder; a red vinyl couch ran the length of each side wall. The large front window advertised Jameson whiskey and the name of the establishment – The Toby Jug – one of a line of businesses along King Street on Dublin's south side.

"First today?" asked the barman.

"No, Simon. Had a couple at lunch."

"Sure, and why not? You're finished with the exams for a bit. And did you get a pass on them, Eric?"

"I did. Grace of God."

"Good for you." Simon topped off the pint and with a wooden spatula whisked away the excess. "So, this one's on the house, Eric. Don't tell the boss."

"Thanks, Simon, your secret is safe. Quarter horses couldn't drag it out of me."

The young man spread his newspaper on the bar, quickly turning the pages looking for news that might have escaped his earlier read. Nothing held his attention for more than a few seconds.

But the stout was good. He could feel its comfort take hold. After a long draught that brought its white collar to mid-glass Eric folded the paper and pushed back from the bar. " Simon," he said, "isn't it peculiar sometimes how things happen? How feckin' fate intrudes in your life, right out of the blue, and when you least expect it?"

"Ah, Jasus, you got that right," Simon replied with a nod. "No rhyme or reason. Inscrutable that fate."

"Like today," Eric continued. "There I was in Hartigan's having a quiet drink, reading the Times. Now you know, Simon, I never go to Hartigan's."

Simon nodded. "Never. The worst pint in Dublin, you always said."

"Still is, by the way. Anyway, there I was reading the paper and there on the front page is a story about a new Minister DeValera brought into his cabinet - a chap named Rourke. I knocked around with his sister, Freda, about a year ago."

"Well," said Simon, his forehead wrinkled, "I wouldn't call that fate. More like a coincidence."

"Let me finish." Eric fished a butted cigarette from his jacket pocket and lighted it. "Anyway, I finish my pint, walk outside and who do I almost knock over?"

Simon chuckled. "Don't tell me. The one herself."

"Herself indeed. Haven't seen her all this time."

"Now," said Simon, beaming at his insight, "that's fate. And you who never go to Hartigan's."

"And if I had stayed for another drink like I was thinking of. The whole thing's just feckin' extraordinary."

Simon shrugged and shook his head, resigned to the lack of explanation.

"Anyway, Eric, looking good was she after the time missing?"

"She was: blue blazer, white turtleneck. Looked a little thinner, otherwise about the same. Always was an attractive bit of goods."

Simon nodded, stubbed out his cigarette, leaned forward, forearms on the bar, a smile broadening his cheeks.

"So, what happened?".

"Anyway," Eric continued, "we hugged. I told her I've missed her, asked what she's been up to. A lot going on in her life, she said, too much to get into right now. She seemed uncomfortable, moving side to side like she wanted to get away. The whole thing was awkward."

"Sounds that way."

"Finally, after some small talk that was going nowhere, I asked her if we could get together. You know a coffee, a drink, for old time sake. No response, Simon, not a glance. She started to leave. So, I cut right to it. 'How about tonight,' I said."

"Good man, Eric. Right to the chase."

"Said she couldn't, she was giving a dinner party. Still wouldn't look at me. So, Simon, I reached over to her and turned her head so she had to face me straight on. It looked like she'd been crying, eyes red and puffy. 'How about after the party,' I asked her. She said something about she couldn't believe meeting like this, today of all days. She wiped her eyes with a handkerchief and finally gave me a little smile. Half eleven would be fine she said, told me her address and walked away. So, Simon, that's where I'll be at midnight tonight."

A voice bellowed at the far end of the bar. "Is it too feckin' much to ask that someone get me a goddamn drink?"

"Right there, sir," says Simon. "Let me know what happens, Eric."

"I will."

Eric ordered another pint, moved to a table in the corner of the lounge, sipped his drink and thought about Freda Rourke. *Do I really want to see this woman, I wondered, a woman who for so long took over my mind, dominated my thoughts until all else was crowded out, school and study forgotten, the desperation when I was not with her, the jealousy, the irrational thoughts, my obsession. I don't want to go through it again, but I have to know what happened, why she disappeared — and why I never was able to win her over.*

Eric Leyden, in spite of his relative youth – his twenty-fourth birth-day recently celebrated – knew he had a way with women. It was not something he worked at, nor did it hint of an immodest arrogance, but just a fact. In the company of men he quickly became bored with their drunken camaraderie. With women, however, he was comfortable, in tune with their thoughts, knowing instinctively what to talk about, how to make them laugh, relaxed in their company even when nothing was being said. With this facility, a winsome smile and a hint of the ne'er-do- well about him he gathered their attention. It was also true: when Eric won over a woman and controlled the romantic battlefield, he, after a short interlude, disengaged and moved on to the next skirmish. Throughout his dating history, that had been his modus operandi - more interested in the campaign than the victory or the occasional setback.

The pub began to fill. Men after work, a couple of students, their classes finished for the day. Eric, with a wave to Simon, headed into the early dusk. There was a chill in the air that sharpened the smell of burning peat. He turned up his collar, thrust his hands deep into the pockets of his jacket and headed home.

They met at a dance hall on Baggot Street near St. Stephens Green on Dublin's south side. In this dimly lit, unadorned hall, the patrons were mainly students and young working types who lived in digs and flats scattered throughout that section of town. A trio led by Humphrey Murphy, a red-faced, rotund piano player with a shock of black hair, provided the music. Lacking ventilation, the space quickly filled with smoke and, as the night progressed, the smell of sweat. Eric was found there most Friday nights after the pubs closed, as he was on that early spring night about a year ago.

Surveying the crowd, checking out the female prospects, Eric noticed a tall woman dancing with a man whose diminished stature limited his gaze to his partner's chin and neck. A woman more attractive than beautiful Eric decided: slim, long blonde hair with a sharply angled face, striking in its pallor. Her outfit: loose white skirt, dark blouse buttoned to the collar, necklace and earrings suited a more fashionable gathering than the rowdy, carelessly garbed lot in attendance. Conversation between the two appeared to be lacking, her fixed smile and frequent glances about the hall signaling boredom. *How did this fragile number end up in this place? A pretty fish in the wrong pond.* On one occasion as they danced past her glance briefly included Eric.

The piano player, hidden behind the dancers in the far corner of the hall, announced the next set would be a lady's choice. A woman headed in Eric's direction then, at the last moment, veered and choose the man next to him. About to move away from the dance area Eric felt a tap on his shoulder. He turned. Beside him was the blonde, as pale up close as she was on the dance floor. "I'm asking you to dance," she said, without smiling, "because you're apparently the only person in this place taller than me."

"I'll take any excuse," Eric answered. Her took her hand and led her to the dance floor. His height was such that their cheeks, although not touching, were within striking distance. As if to establish her social credentials, she mentioned she was here to meet a friend, her tone implying that the choice of rendezvous was unfortunate. Eric asked her name. Leaning toward her for the response, her hair, trailing a soft fragrance, brushed his cheek.

"Freda Rourke."

"I've never met a Freda."

"And you're?"

"Eric."

His stabs at small talk failed to elicit either a smile or anything beyond a couple of words in response. But she seemed comfortable, danced well, hummed along with the melody, but, like the plight of the little man earlier, paid scant attention to her partner.

The first song of the set ended. Her willingness, at Eric's suggestion, to remain on the floor for another go-around seemed more a courtesy than a measure of interest This time, however, the space between them narrowed slightly. Brief contact was made with her cheek. Snippets of conversation achieved some length.

In defense of his shabby appearance: stained white shirt, wrinkled khakis, worn jacket and redolent of stout and butted cigarettes, Eric mentioned she looked great but too well dressed for this crowd. Although now with the top two buttons of her blouse undone for cooling purposes she looked less the chaste choir girl seen earlier.

"Didn't know what to expect. My friend didn't warn me. So, Eric, you come here a lot?"

"Yeh, the pub I use is just down the street. So, it's handy. Not too far to stagger."

A small smile – the first – registered on her face. As she offered reasons why she preferred the tennis club dances: less crowded, bigger bands, better songs - the set ended. She thanked him for the dances, adding that since her friend hadn't appeared she was going home. "It's just too hot and crowded here."

"Where do you live?"

"Just beyond Fitzwilliam Square."

"Why don't I walk you home? I was thinking of leaving myself."

A flash of irritation crossed her face. She shrugged her shoulders. "Guess it would be all right." *Probably wasting my time with this one, Eric thought, but, hell, it's worth a try. Nothing ventured… as they say.*

Within two blocks they were past the commercial edge of town – darkened buildings and small shops – then followed a line of three decker houses into a more upscale residential area. She mentioned – her tone more relaxed, less haughty – that she liked where she lived, "quiet and handy to the bus line." Freda told of her move from Donegal a month earlier and her present job as manager in a Dublin hotel - both good decisions she felt.

Away from the music and the thrash of conversations at the dance hall her north of Ireland accent became apparent. Her voice had a husky, breathless quality that – when accompanied by a laugh – sounded slightly off key. "No I don't have a cold," she said, "I always sound this way. Except when I get mad. Then it's more of a screech."

They reached a major intersection. As they passed beneath a fluorescent light, Eric glanced at her profile: the slender neck, the sharp angular face, her cheeks lost in shadow. Sensing his look, she turned, her blonde hair bathed in an orange glow swept across her shoulders, her eyes heavy- lidded with a questioning look. She smiled. The effect was immediate and sensual.

On reaching her neighborhood the night had cooled - the breeze sharp on his face. Mist had gathered beneath the string of trees on each side of the street and the roadway glistened in the glare of car lights. Her flat was in one of a series of Georgian-style brick dwellings; heavy, black rails and gates guarded their entrances and the small squares of lawn. She recognized her place from the others, she said, by the polished brass plate in the center of its front door. A series of steps led to a lower door, the entrance to her flat; her preference, she said, because of the privacy and separate entrance.

Eric's attempt to kiss her was deflected, her hand cold and firm on his face. However, she agreed to meet the following night. She had been given tickets for a film playing at the Corinthian cinema in Dublin, which she was interested in seeing but preferred not to attend alone. "I'm sure," she added, "you will enjoy it also, if you don't mind sub-titles."

The lights of the theatre lobby softened but could not disguise her fragile features; skin drawn so tight about her cheeks as to be almost translucent. But, damn, she did look good in that teal sweater and hip-hugging skirt. The kiss on his cheek was brief and polite. "Thank you for being prompt."

The film, a French flick, included, along with a byzantine plot, a beach scape of braless women interspersed with snippets of their bed room antics with well-endowed, muscular men. Imagination was required as to what actually occurred, as the film was fast-forwarded through the risqué interludes.

Discussing the movie later, Eric talked about the censorship: "After a while, with all the interruptions, you lose track of the story." Freda explained that the Church censors all films. "They don't want their young men to become more excitable than they already are. We've got too many kids in the country already. Here we are in 1958," she said, "and, as I'm sure you know, Eric, we still have no birth control."

Two meetings with Freda over the next fortnight ended with a thank you and a hurried kiss. On the third occasion Eric decided to find out one way or the other if something more satisfying was on the horizon. If not, chalk it up to experience and move on.

"Freda," he began, "we get along pretty well. Agreed?"

Her response – an enigmatic smile.

"I'll take your silence as a yes. But I'd like to know you better. It's frustrating, you know, not being able to show it a little more."

"Really," she said, her voice teasing. She took his hands. "It's sex you're talking about, Eric, and I really don't want to get into it just yet."

"But..."

"Let me finish," she said. "I'm a virgin and intend to stay that way until I'm married. Though we've gotten along well so far, that's not likely for us. Nor do I wish to get pregnant. Do you agree?"

Eric nodded yes. "But," he added, "there are other things. Hell, even a bottle of wine and listen to music. Stuff like that."

A light went on in a second-story window. A shade was pulled down. She dropped his hands and walked a few steps out of viewing range.

Yes," she said, her voice lowered. "I know very well. And maybe we can begin to know each other better. We'll see. But whatever we do it will be my choice. That may not suit you. And I don't want you to become violent or depressed or whatever men do when they don't get their way."

"I guess I can live with that."

"Well, then, come by tomorrow night. Around eight would be good."

Eric's arrival the next evening was greeted with a hug, which he felt was encouraging. The apartment wasn't large: studio size, with a couch, one stuffed chair and a bed placed kitty-corner next to the bathroom. A wooden counter extending from the wall separated the kitchenette from the remaining space. Over the bed was a framed picture of the Virgin Mary; another wall displayed a portrait of Eamon DeValera, Ireland's Prime Minister. Next to the bed was a small table with a lamp, radio, a box of tissues and rosary beads.

"Make yourself comfortable," she said, nodding toward the couch. She went behind the counter and returned with a bottle of white wine and two glasses. A long, white robe tied loosely at the waist allowed glimpses of long pale legs, which she tucked beneath her when she joined him on the couch.

The wine was dry and good. Their conversation, which began with politics, flowed easily. She was harsh in her condemnation of the Fine Gael party in the upcoming election but confident that DeValera – and her brother who had a post in the government – would maintain their present positions in Fianna Fail. She mentioned a retreat to Lourdes planned for late summer. That, her third trip, would be her first experience as a litter bearer, transporting the sick to the baths.

When she leaned forward to refill his glass, her robe slipped from a shoulder. As she reached for it, Eric took her hand and pulled her toward him.

She resisted. "You do remember what I said last night, don't you?"

"I do."

"Well, nothing has changed." She paused a moment, as though considering her next words, then continued. "However, as you mentioned, there are other ways we can please each other. But only if done my way. Do you understand?"

Her tone was brisk and impersonal. It reminded Eric of a counselor about to rattle off the rules at a summer camp he attended as young boy.

He shrugged his shoulders. "Fine."

"First," she said, "you take a bath. You must have a pleasant smell and be very clean. I have a thing about that."

"But I'm already…"

"Please," she interrupted. "You can take as much time as you like. Bring the wine with you. I've already put fragrance in the tub."

The tub was small. Eric couldn't straighten his legs. But the water was abundant and hot, unlike the tepid, sparse supply offered in his digs. *If I get nothing more out of this night than the wine and bath I'm ahead of the game.*

Warm and fragrant, a towel around his waist, Eric emerged from the bathroom. The room, now lighted by a line of candles along the counter, had a scent of musk that he hadn't noticed before.

Freda finished what was left of her wine and came to him. She pulled the towel away. "I'll finish the drying." As she made her way – neck,

71

then chest – she nipped the skin with her teeth, small bites that stung for a few seconds, then cleared. As she leaned toward his belly her robe opened; she straightened, pushed it from her shoulders, let it fall to the floor, then backed away.

Her body bathed in candle glow belied the thinness of her face. Breasts, shadowed mounds, were full, a narrow waist flared to broad hips and thighs, imposing columns of white in the dimness.

"Look all right?" she asked.

"Very all right."

Freda took the rosary beads from the bedside table and, after blessing herself, slipped them over her head, the cross nestled between her breasts. She switched on the small light by the bed, then went to a closet by the front door. She returned with what in the semi-darkness looked like a leather strap, the type used by barbers to sharpen razors; at one end was a leather handle, at the other a silver ball the size of a small Christmas tree ornament.

She handed the strap to Eric. "I want to be whipped," she said simply.

"You got to be kidding."

"No, I'm going to lie on the bed and you're going to lash me."

"You know, Freda," he stammered, "I...I don't know about this." *What in hell's going on here? What have I gotten myself into with this crazy woman?*

"You agreed. Whatever we did would be my choice. Anyway, who knows, you might enjoy it. Let's see what happens."

She handed Eric the strap, dialed the radio to a music station, increased the volume and pushed the pillows on the floor. Face down on the bed Freda hooked her fingers around the head board, then turned toward Eric. "Now, you can start," she said, "not too hard at first. But if I tell you to stop then you do."

Tentatively he began, then harder and faster in response to her urgings. The skin on her back began to darken, welts started to form. Sweat burned his eyes, breathing bordered on a pant. He felt pressure beginning to build. "Yes, yes that's good," her voice a deep growl. "Don't stop." She loosened a hand and slid it below her belly.

Her hips jerked from side to side. "Harder," she moaned, "don't..." Then a scream. Her back arched. The sight brought Eric an exquisite urgency. He exploded the leather strap across her raised, glistening backside. "Oh, sweet, sweet Jesus," she cried. She looked up at the crucifix, blessed herself, then fell back onto the bed. Eric dropped the strap and fell beside her, burrowing his head into the sheets. Far off a song about a "white sports coat and a pink carnation" was playing.

A bell tolled eleven o'clock far off in the night. Eric's eyes were shut. Sleep was approaching. He felt a jab in his ribs. "Don't get too comfortable, my friend, fair's fair and I do keep my promises. I need to use the loo right now. But when I get back let's see what I can do for you."

And, so it began and continued sporadically over the next few months. In spite of frequent trips up north, back to Donegal – and the pilgrimage to Lourdes – she maintained her position at the hotel. The absences, she explained, were related to "family things and retreats."

Their dates followed a familiar pattern: a meeting at a bar, some drinks – she liked dry white wine – and a return to her place where, with some refinements, they began her preferred courting activity. Eric, though not an especially ardent sort, was struck by how impersonal were their get-togethers. None of the romantic niceties – kisses, sentiments of affection – were offered prior to the main event – nor after. That was fine with him. just different.

Freda valued her privacy, Eric learned, and was hesitant to confide anything of her free-time activities. She spoke of her family – her mother at some length, her father hardly a mention, growing up in Letterkenny with her older brother, but the telling was brief, free of anecdote and childhood reminiscences. After some probing she admitted having two relationships during her twenty-one years but nothing longer than a few months. "Do you believe me?" she asked, her tone playful. Eric said he did, but, on her return from a trip away, he always checked her body for any fresh bruising. Nothing suspicious was ever found.

As their relationship continued Eric became aware of a change in his behavior, which was not only unfamiliar but disturbing: He had begun to enjoy the beatings he inflicted on Freda, to the extent he was occasionally reluctant to desist in spite of her pleas. Whether there was some transference of her sexual excitement to him or a deep-seated hostility toward women playing out he wasn't sure. But the escalating sadistic tendency bothered him. Although certain his urges could be contained in their present situation, he wondered what his reaction might be if he found she was involved with another man.

That spring Freda took the position of manager at a hotel in Bray, a seaside resort, twelve miles south of Dublin. Eric visited on weekends. The occasional mid-week tryst necessitated an early wake-up the following day for morning classes. Eventually, fatigue and missed trains forced the decision to meet only weekends.

That summer, they both agreed, were their best times. The five -day separation had its benefits: a chance for Eric to catch up on neglected studies, refresh his libido and allow Freda's bruises to fade.

On arrival Saturday night, Eric socialized with guests and locals in the hotel bar until Freda finished work around nine. A room - which included the luxury of a shower – had been arranged which, if available, would be the honeymoon suite. Since they both enjoyed dancing and if Freda felt up to it, migraine headaches were a frequent visitor dependent on the stress level of her day, they headed to the ballroom of the Arcadia Hotel. The venue, crowded on summer weekends, featured a house band whose offerings included mainly American and English songs. If in a playful mood, Freda might request "Mr. Wonderful" – a popular song at the time – which the band leader announced was being played for Eric – to his acute embarrassment. Her body tight to his, their lips brushing, she whispered the lyric:

> *Why this feeling? Why this glow?*
> *Why his thrill when you say hello?*
> *It's a strange and tender magic you do,*
> *Mr. Wonderful that's you.*

Some nights after the dance, if the moon was especially bright, they walked the boardwalk along the beach. It was on one of those nights that

Eric learned the beginnings of her attachment to Jesus, the Blessed Mother, and the offerings of pain she made to them.

"It all began in secondary school," she began. "I was a pretty good student but always in trouble. Making faces behind the teacher's back, pulling the hair of the girl sitting in front of me, erasing the alphabet along the top of the blackboard when Sister wasn't around. Anything to get attention, and I could pretty much get away with it." Her family, she explained, was prominent in town and generous to the church.

"Anyway, one day Sister Constance, my seventh-grade teacher, had her fill. Her face got so red I thought she was going to have a stroke. I've forgotten what I did but she came after me with a ruler. She made me put my hands out in front of me, palms down, and began hitting them. The more she hit the harder I laughed. She was furious. I told her I liked it. That wasn't true at the time, but Sister looked at me sort of strange and stopped. Said she'd talk to me later."

"And did she?"

"Yes, I didn't know what to expect. It was a strange conversation. After she asked me a few more questions she started talking about pain, that it was necessary for salvation. We should seek it out, embrace it, offer it up. Even Jesus, Sister said, had to go through the experience. That was the purpose of the passion: the crown of thorns, the nails in His hands and feet, the torture, all necessary, even for Him, to see His Father in heaven."

"That's one weird nun, Freda." *But I'm sure it's true. The Christian Brothers in my high school sure didn't spare the cane or the back of their hand to enforce discipline Our salvation was hardly a consideration.*

"I think she wanted me to become a Sister. She told me about an order of nuns who inflict pain on themselves, wear belts with nails in them, strap themselves, stuff like that."

"Did she want to do something to you?"

"No, but she did change. Nice to me in class. Like she wanted me to be her friend."

"So, she got you thinking."

"Yes, I always was a religious kid, comfortable talking to the Blessed Mother about my problems, More than Jesus or God Himself. Maybe because they were men. After that, every time I felt discomfort I offered it to Mary as penance for bad thoughts, you know, like swearing, thinking about boys, family stuff."

"And then there was the sex part."

"Yeh, I got a kid who liked me – a real jerk actually – to hit me with a belt. I had my clothes on. He thought it was stupid and boring but went along with it. Somewhere along the line I discovered that pain and me touching myself felt good. I never mentioned it to Sister. I often wondered if she did it also."

"What happened to her?"

"I don't know. One day she wasn't at school. The principal said she was transferred."

They stopped at the end of the boardwalk and settled into one of the fixed seats along its length. The sea was calm, its inky blackness lightened by a full moon scurrying between a jumble of clouds. The tide was low and the off-shore breeze smelled of salt, its moisture fresh on their skin.

Eric put his arm around her. She turned to him. The dampness had formed a line of ringlets across her brow.

"Moonlight becomes you, my dear," he shook his head. "How I'd love to know what lurks behind that beautiful face, the Mona Lisa smile. Get to meet your demons."

"If you knew it all, Eric, there would be nothing left to wonder. Nothing to keep you interested. Perhaps you wouldn't like me then."

"Maybe not. But I'd take the chance." He grinned and dabbed a drop of moisture from the tip of her nose. "The way things are going now I just hope I survive. "

"Me too."

One Sunday late that summer they climbed, as they often did, the rocky face of Brayhead, a modest headland jutting into the Irish sea; they had planned a picnic before their trek through the adjacent Wicklow mountains. A flat swath of grass was found that overlooked the water, a lilac color in the afternoon light. The Dun Laoghhaire ferry was passing, en route to England, the passengers waving to those on the shore. The contents of Eric's backpack – sandwiches, fruit, a bottle of wine

– accompanied nicely their lazy conversation. Warmed by the mid-day sun, their bellies full, the mood good, they began their wander through the wooded foothills.

Freda, by her own account, was not an outdoor person but enjoyed walking, especially in the solitude of a forest where she felt "close to God." On occasion she stopped along the trail and listened to "God's whispers," as she called the murmur of the winds tacking through the tall trees. "We mustn't move," she said softly, "until we hear a sound." So, they remained quiet and still until the chirp of a bird or the dash of a rabbit broke the silence. Then they continued on.

As the evening faded into the long summer twilight, they found a clearing. Stretched out on the soft grass, surrounded by a circle of trees, puffs of white clouds in the window of blue above, the backpack their pillow, they talked of many things. Freda delighted in recollecting the myths of Ireland, of Tir Non Og, of Grainne and Brian, of Tara and the ancient Kings. She recited patches of verse in Gaelic, its harsh cadence softened by the breathless quality of her voice. The stories were meaningless to Eric; their beauty lay not with the words, but in the sound and rhythm of the verse.

As she finished one of the stories, her eyes filled, her voice trailed off, and she began to cry softly. When Eric wondered what was wrong she shook her head. "Nothing," she said, her voice thick. "Just me, my craziness and this beautiful moment." With a tenderness new to him Eric held her, and, as one would a frightened child, kissed away her tears. He had never seen Freda so exposed, so fragile – nor himself for that matter.

However, as vulnerable as Freda appeared and as opportune the moment, Eric's tentative suggestions of love were dismissed by a shake of her head.

"Why not," he persisted. "What more does it take? Tell me," he asked, his voice edged with frustration. "Have you ever really been in love with anyone in your life?"

Freda stood, brushed away grass that clung to her clothes, ran her fingers through her hair and looked at her watch. The breeze had calmed, the trees were quiet, far off came the dull drone of the sea.

"Just once. The love a young girl has for her father." She paused. "For me it bordered on adoration."

Eric frowned. "I didn't mean that, but I suppose there is something special with fathers and daughters, a bond that's hard to break."

"Yes, it was – for a long while," Freda paused. "But it didn't turn out well."

"What happened?"

"That's something I don't talk about. Let's just say I was devastated by a man who meant the world to me. But I learned a lesson."

"What's that?

"Never love anyone that you can't bear to lose."

"But maybe with us it will be different."

"We will never find out." She smiled and took his hand. "But if it were to happen, even if I could feel it coming on, I wouldn't allow it."

"What would you do?"

"Run away."

"That's stupid."

Freda smiled and started back along the trail, the trees in shadow, the path barely visible. She stopped and turned. "Don't be so serious. my dear. This thing we have will one day leave us, and as some poet said, 'flee into the heavens and hide in the circus of stars.'"

"Oh, that's just bullshit," he said, his voice laced with annoyance.

"You're right, Eric. Just Irish palaver. So, don't be upset."

But he was.

And so their romance continued through the summer. Freda was enjoying her work at the hotel. Eric's weekend visits were relaxed and mutually enjoyed. In fact, there was a warming of the relationship. Hugs had become commonplace, her kisses more freely given. Phone calls to him setting up plans for the upcoming weekend were another new development. Perversely, the turnabout only increased his suspicions. *She's up to something, this is just a cover.*

The uncertainty began to affect his ability to function. Daily activities became annoying distractions, conversations hurried along so he could return to thoughts of her, sleep was interrupted, appetite gone, weight lost. Studying required an extraordinary effort. The days were counted until they were together again.

When they met, Eric disguised his vulnerability with playful banter and a carefree demeanor, a facade of disinterest. Casually, he would ask her what she had been up to, her answers carefully parsed for hints that might suggest involvement with another man. When she was naked, he, as always, carefully examined her body for fresh marks. And, to his chagrin, no matter in what guise Eric framed the question, and in spite of her increased warmth, she never indicated their relationship was anything more than friendship. Sometimes he wanted to beat her until she told him what he wanted to hear but realized a forced confession was worse than silence.

Eric knew he was becoming emotionally unhinged. Frightened by his thoughts, racked by jealousy and gnawing distrust, he knew he couldn't go on like this – but he also knew he couldn't stop.

Then one day Freda was gone.

After a fortnight, she was still gone. Her landlady and employer had no clue where she was. Eric would have written but she had never divulged her home address. "I'm just the girl from Donegal," was her standard, waggish reply. The days became weeks, then months, still no contact -- until today and the serendipitous collision outside Hartigan's pub.

Her apartment – which faced St. Stephen's Green – was disheveled: plates, dishes, silverware, wine glasses were scattered over a table, centered by a candelabra of extinguished candles, and covered with a stained white tablecloth, chairs and furniture in random disarray. The smells of cooking remained; one window was partially open, its curtain pulled aside. Freda greeted him with a hug and remarked on his good timing; the guests had left about a half-hour earlier.

Their conversation to begin was stilted, becoming easier somewhere between the leftover wine and the gin and tonics. Reminiscences were relished. Eric was delighted to hear again her husky voice deepen to laughter. The cool disinterest he adopted was maintained through the first round of drinks but didn't survive the second.

"So, tell me, Freda, where have you been? Not even a goodbye to an old friend. That wasn't very nice."

They were seated facing each other on a faded yellow couch, the armrests worn and discolored. Freda had lost weight, the sharp angles of her face even more chiseled. A black shawl draped over her shoulders accentuated her paleness. There seemed a weariness about her, an uneasy emptiness in her eyes, the look of someone who needed a vacation or a few nights of uninterrupted sleep.

"I don't know if I could have said goodbye face to face. You see, Eric, you were the reason I left. We were getting on very well, too well. It was time to go."

"I'd like to believe that, Freda, and right now I'm mellow enough that I will." She declined another drink. Eric refreshed his, finishing the gin in the process.

"So, with the person you like so much not around," he asked, the sarcasm evident, "what did you do with yourself?"

"Oh, a lot has happened. I'll explain it all. But it can wait for now. I'm just glad to see you, although I didn't want to. You take me back to a better place," she said with a smile. "We really did have a marvelous summer, didn't we, the walks in the woods, the picnics, the dances." She laughed. "And, of course, the bridal suite. And you, how are you doing? School going well?"

"Pretty good since you disappeared. Yeh, I'm doing all right."

The idle chatter continued. Eric began to feel, in spite of her friendliness and up-beat manner, the banter was forced, a fandango meant to obscure, clouding, perhaps, an issue she wished to avoid. Time, he thought, to get a little down and dirty, cut through the bullshit, find out what's going on.

"Did I tell you about my trip to Lourdes?" she continued. "I've forgotten if I had. Anyway, it was..."

"Freda."

"Yes."

"I've missed you,"

She smiled. "How much?"

"Very much."

"And not just my lips," her tone teasing.

"Much more." The lightness in his voice was gone. He took her hands and pulled her to him. "But perhaps we can refresh the recollection."

A church bell tolled far off in the night. An unseen moon cast its dull light on the wooden floor. An occasional gust of wind rattled the shutters.

"You haven't lost your touch."

She responded with a husky laugh. "Somehow I knew that."

"But fair is fair, as you say. Let me do something for you."

She shook her head. "We can't do those things anymore. And, certainly not now."

"How come? What's going on?"

She got up from the couch, walked to the half-open window and stood there silent and unmoving, her gaze fixed on the empty street.

"Well?"

Freda drew the curtains together, turned and faced him. "I'm getting married."

Eric sat up as if jolted. "Married?" He paused. "You're putting me on, right?"

"No. I'm not," she said. "Wish I was."

"What are you talking about? When?"

She sat beside him. The hands that sought his were cold and shaking. "Tomorrow morning at 10 o'clock."

Eric switched on the side table lamp and looked at her. Tears streaked her cheeks, face blotchy, eyes puffy.

"You're not kidding, then? Not a big joke?"

"It's a joke all right, but a joke that is scheduled to happen…" She looked at her watch. "In about eight hours. And, here I am with you."

"Talk to me."

She drew the shawl tightly about her, took a sip of his drink, and began. After leaving Dublin she found work up north at a hotel near her hometown. Over the course of a few weeks a man who drank there most nights took a fancy to her. He came from a well-to-do family, socially connected to hers but unknown to Freda. "It was all very innocent at first," she said, "and I paid him no attention. But soon he was ringing me up two or three times a week, pleading with me to go out with him. More to stop the phone calls, I agreed to meet him. I had absolutely no interest in him."

A wave of nausea washed over Eric, his face suddenly warm, hands sweaty, fists clenched. *I knew it, I knew she was seeing someone else.* He didn't dare look at her, afraid what he might say or do.

"I met him socially three times, twice in the hotel bar after work and once we went to a birthday party. Nothing happened. Each time he got very drunk, maudlin drunk. He told me he had been waiting for me all his life, wanted to marry me. He was like a little puppy licking my hand. But, he was a mean drinker, would say cruel things. Coming home from the birthday party he hit me. He was full of apologies the next day but I stopped seeing him. He still came to the hotel most nights but I would have nothing to do with him."

The sky was beginning to lighten, the occasional blare of a car horn punctuated the quiet. Eric stood up, went to the open window, stuck his head outside and took some deep breaths. He felt sick. Stomach juices, oozing from the sides of his mouth, were spit onto the sidewalk below. Hands on the sill, he waited for the vomit. Nothing, the cold air had taken the edge off. He turned and looked at Freda tucked into the corner of the couch.

"And you're the one that told me all that shit how you would never love anyone again, never get married, you would run away first. And me, the fool, believing you!"

"That's still the truth. I don't love him. Never have."

"Then tell me," Eric said, his voice hard, face flushed with anger, "why you are feck'n marrying him?"

"I will as soon as you stop shouting."

Eric brought a hard-backed chair from the dining area, placed it in front of the couch and sat down. "Okay, tell your story. Let's hear the fairy tale. Let's hear the lies."

"Are you finished?"

Eric shrugged. "Talk, get it over with."

"All right then." Tucking her legs beneath her she began. "One night at the hotel just before the bar closed, Aidan, that's his first name, left the lounge and headed to the men's room. As he crossed the lobby he fell. I heard the crash and went to see what happened; he was lying on the floor, trying to stand up. He tried to push himself up. His hand slipped. He cracked his face on the floor. The blood ran down his face onto his shirt. He looked over at me with those sad eyes. 'See what you've done,' he said. 'Please, in the name of God, take me back.' Then he started to cry. By then one of the off-duty waiters was there to help him.

"I stood and watched. It was such a pitiful sight. Then I began to think, perhaps it is God's will. Maybe I was put here to help this poor, unfortunate soul."

"You really expect me to buy this crap. Like God decided to trip him. That's what you really want me to believe?"

"Why not? If we hadn't met today at the exact second we did you wouldn't be here tonight."

Eric gave a dismissive shrug of his shoulders. "Strange things happen sometimes."

"They do. But I'm certain of one thing … we were destined to meet today."

"Well, I don't know what purpose it served. But you still haven't told me why you're marrying the guy."

"Well, while the waiter went to call an ambulance I went over to him. It was eerie, almost like I was being directed. I told him if he stopped drinking for six months I'd marry him. He made me promise. And I did. I swore on the name of the Blessed Mother. And, Eric, he hasn't had a drink since. He became a new man, loving, thoughtful and caring. Our families were delighted. But I don't want to marry him. There's no desire for him in my body. My promise was made out of pity. Nothing more." She paused. "Deep down I'm frightened. And our meeting today? It happened so you could save me from him. I'm totally convinced of that."

Eric looked at her. Her eyes were fixed on his. She was dead serious. "So, how do you propose I do that?"

"I've got two tickets to Paris for tonight. Come with me."

Eric looked at her. "Have you forgotten your 10 o'clock appointment?"

"Listen to me. I'll tell him I met someone who convinced me I was making a mistake or that God had spoken to me in a dream or that I didn't have any feeling for him. I'll think of an excuse to stop it."

"You're talking crazy stuff, Freda."

She took his hands. "It will only be for a few days. Everything is all set. We have hotel reservations. And when he finds out I'm with another man, he'll never take me back. Please Eric, I beg you. You will save my life."

"I'm tempted to do it," he answered, "just for the craic of it all. But this is serious stuff."

Eric stood, put on his jacket and headed for the door. "So, thanks but no thanks, as they say." He stopped and turned toward her. "But you can tell me one thing before I go." Eric paused. "And be honest."

"Yes."

"Did you ever give a shit about me, did you ever love me?"

"You'll never know."

"Never know what?"

"You just will never know."

Eric grabbed her by the shoulders and shook her. "Know what? Goddamn it. Tell me. I need you to tell me."

"Stop, you're hurting me." She took his hands and held them; tears spilled down her face. "I loved you as much as I was able." Her voice choked on the tears. "And then there's the other thing."

"What's that?"

"I didn't want to lose you."

"Why would you?"

"Once you had me, were in control, you'd be gone with the tide."

Eric shook his head and smiled. "You, Freda Rourke, are an Irish witch. You're probably right. But we'll never know, will we?" He buttoned his jacket. "One thing for sure, I'm not going to be happy with you being with another man."

She put her arms around his neck. "Then, come with me tonight." She paused, the slightest of smiles flitted over her face. "Mr. Wonderful?"

Eric chuckled. "A little late, my dear. But keep the thought."

Her cheek was wet against his. A hint of perfume remained. Her lips tasted of tears.

Eric leaned against the iron grates of Stephens Green, opposite the Newman Chapel. Cars were lined the length of the street. A chauffeur was standing next to a limousine flying the Irish national flag, parked at the chapel door. Probably a government vehicle, Eric thought; he lit a cigarette and waited.

Bells soon began to chime; the wedding party started to file out. The outfits of the bridesmaids, favored by a sparkling sun, were a collage of yellows and greens. Then he saw her, pale and beautiful in a flowing white gown, the train carried by two small boys.

A square, florid man, tuxedo tight around his chest, shorter than his bride, was accepting congratulations from all sides. As she stepped into the limousine, Freda looked toward the Green and saw Eric. A smile crossed her face and, as if adjusting her veil, raised her hand and blew a kiss. Eric returned a small salute. Then she was gone.

Eric watched the limousine pull away, then found a bench in the park where he sat, smoked cigarettes and thought about Freda Rourk. The bravado of the previous hours was gone, replaced with a sense of loss and regret. Eric didn't want it to end, certainly not with a shouting match or the casualness of a wind-blown kiss. A glass of wine, hands being held, a lazy reminiscence of the good times would have been a more civilized coda. A chat that reconciled the differences and soothed the hurt feelings each had inflicted on the other would befit the moment. They would, perhaps, resolve not to meet again but be available to offer each other support. Eric also knew – considering the personalities involved – that such rational ambitions were improbable. However, for the sake of his sanity, Eric was determined to resolve the madness one way or the other. How – considering today's activities – was the question.

Leaving the Green Eric glanced at the chapel across the street. Flowers flung at the newlyweds when they exited the chapel were scattered on the sidewalk. Retrieving one – a small, white carnation – Eric secured it in his lapel and resumed his stroll down the street. Reaching the corner, he looked up at the apartment where they were last night. The window was still open, its curtain ballooned by the breeze. He shook his head. *It's almost as though I imagined it all.*

A note, which included a return address, arrived six weeks later:

Dearest,

I saw you by the Green, my heart cried. It's been a terrible mistake. He's into the drink again. And the meanness. I'm frightened.
Pray for me.

Always,
Freda

Eric sent a letter proposing a reunion. By return post, Freda indicated her agreement but wouldn't be able to manage an "escape" for a fortnight. She would be in touch by mail.

As promised, a note was received that informed him of the time, place and directions to their assignation. A few days later Eric boarded the Belfast train at Westland Row station with connections to Donegal.

Eric blotted the stout running down the glass on the newspaper lying on the bar. It had been a few weeks since he last raised a pint at the Toby. Not because he had lost his taste for the drink. Hardly; rather a required two-month residency in an inner-city hospital had taken him out of Toby Jug range.

"So how are things going?" asked Simon, putting a coaster under the pint. "Good to have you back in circulation. See you've started a beard."

"Yeh, always wanted to try one. Been hiking up North for a few days, no point in shaving. Pretty scruffy right now. You been good?"

"Too good," laughed Simon. "That's my problem. But one thing I've been wanting to ask you."

"What's that?"

"How you made out with the bird you bumped into that day? You know, the old girlfriend in front of Hartigans, a while back it was now."

"Oh sure, I remember. Yeh, we went out for a while but she started getting serious, you know how that goes. So, I had to dump her. I understand she went off and got married." Eric paused. "Three months this past Saturday."

"Ah well, they come and they go."

Eric took a long pull of his pint, stubble masking a rueful smile. *Except the ones who go but never leave, say goodbye but don't depart. The one who stays stuck in your head and makes you crazy.*

The Irish Times

BRUTAL MURDER IN DONEGAL

September 5, 1959 DONEGAL – Freda Scanlan, missing for three days, was found in dense underbrush last evening by two fisherman as they walked along the shore of Lake Swilley. The body, unclothed, was badly bruised. Rosary beads were knotted tightly around her neck. A fierce struggle was presumed as human skin was lodged beneath her fingernails. Married just three months, her husband, Brandon, vowed to find the perpetrators. Mr. Scanlan was also questioned in regard to superficial scratches noted on his face, which he attributed to clearing fallen limbs on their farm. He will be questioned again after an appropriate interval. A cottage near the murder will be examined for signs of recent habitation. The family of the deceased (*continued page A6*)

The murder was reported on the front page of all the major newspapers, including the one next to Eric at the bar. Even though the article was outlined by a circle of stout, he failed to notice it. Perhaps he didn't have to. Perhaps he already knew.

9

THE GOLFING FATHER

MY CADDY EXPERIENCE AT THE Point Judith Country Club (PJCC) began when I was thirteen years old. At that time – in the early 1950's – the majority of the membership were relatives and friends of the original twenty-five owners who, in 1894, established the facility. The prevailing demographic: white, Anglo-Saxon and Protestant.

In order to provide funding for the operation of the club, without unduly sullying its ethnic purity, certain of the local population — bank president, school superintendent and prominent businessmen – were allowed membership. This gesture did not include use of the clubhouse. Shoe and wardrobe changes were accomplished in the parking lot.

Among the acceptable cohort was Father John Sallesses, the pastor at Saint Philomena's Catholic church (now Saint Thomas More), in Narragansett. My association with the good father, although pleasant in every respect, came with an unfortunate asterisk.

"Guess who I caddied for today," was a question I frequently asked my family on my return from the course, especially if it was a prominent politician or a well-known businessman. In spite of the generous clues I provided, few guessed correctly. "Okay," someone would say. "We give up, who?" On this summer afternoon the answer was Father Sallesses.

My family attended Mass at St. Philomena's and were great fans of the pastor. Accordingly, the ensuing conversation only underscored my good fortune having worked for such a "lovely man". Then came the dagger courtesy of my kindly, gray-haired grandmother, of all people.

"You know, Gene," she began, "you shouldn't take money from him." The tone of her voice had more the ring of an edict, less that of a suggestion.

"Why not?"

"Because he's a priest, a man of God. Taking the little money he has would be like robbing the poor. And that is a mortal sin."

In that era most of the Catholic kids I knew – in preparation for weekly confession – were instructed to make a list of their venial and mortal sins for recitation to the priest in the confessional. Those in the mortal column were the most grievous. For starters they came with an automatic penance of ten Our Fathers and ten Hail Marys, with the potential of an entire rosary — and a possible talking-to by the man himself, often enjoying a cigarette behind the screen.

"How about the tip?" I asked.

"That, too, of course."

I nodded and remained quiet. My grandmother, although generally an affable lady, could, on occasion, become crotchety. What might be a difference of opinion from an adult often became "back talk" from a teenager. It was best not to test the distinction.

The next time I was on Father's bag I told him of the decree from the homefront. He was visibly delighted, his usual benevolent expression expanding into a broad grin. The gratitude that animated his face seemed less the look of a man of the cloth and more of a poker player who had just filled an inside straight.

"Bless you my son. And your family. You all are in my prayers." He placed a hand on my head and mumbled something that sounded like Latin.

As a result of this unfortunate charity I did my best to avoid jobs with Father, but the caddy master – a son of Italy and also a Catholic – couldn't ignore the wishes of his parish priest. Father would call mid-morning and reserve me for later that day. This effectively took me out of a high-paying afternoon job. But I was assured by my folks that someday God would reward my good deed. A half century has passed. *Anytime now Lord would be good. No rush. Just sayin'.*

Father seldom played in the organized four ball matches, rather making his appearance late afternoons playing either by himself or with a fellow priest. Father loved the game of golf, but his affection – and heavenly connections – didn't translate into notable excursions on the course. As Billy Graham reportedly said, "The only time my prayers are never answered is on the golf course" – a sentiment to which Father Sallesses might add an appreciative "Amen."

However, Father's lack of expertise mattered little to him. His enjoyment of the game, he often said, came from being out on a splendid summer evening strolling the lush green fairways surrounded by abundant nature. "If I hit a few good shots along the way all the better."

Often, he would sit for a few minutes at a tee-side bench and absorb the scene – the darkening expanse of green, the pastels of the day in retreat, shadows lengthening behind the fairway bunkers. The stops, I noticed, were often made when Father was having trouble catching his breath. I wondered if more was going on than simply an appreciation of his surroundings.

Portly, and of medium height, white hair ringing a mostly bald scalp, Father seemed to be in his sixties. Somewhat lost in the gentle folds of his pale face were blue eyes that took on a glint of mischief when he smiled. His soft voice, gentle manner and unwavering kindness fit my perception perfectly of a holy man, an image enhanced when wearing his "work clothes."

The man who said Mass at 7:00 o'clock on Sunday morning, resplendent in vestments encrusted with gold and other vibrant colors, scarcely resembled the man I might be caddying for later that day. A pair of baggy khakis, hitched up by a belt always missing at least one loop, a long sleeved white shirt sporting a Hawaiian design and a faded Boston Red Sox cap was his usual golfing ensemble. Although certainly appropriate, the outfit was a striking contrast to the raiment worn earlier in the day.

Other than the financial hit, I enjoyed my rounds with Father. We got along well. Since he seemed to tire easily, we maintained a comfortable meander around the course, usually abbreviated to ten holes. His shots, never of great distance, were always straight, so lost balls were never a problem. And he always had a stout supply of hard candy that he willingly shared.

Father liked his quiet. Lengthy conversations didn't intrude during our round. The clue that signaled the retreat to his own space: the sound of gentle humming. Two or three holes could be played with only the barest of communication. Often his lips were moving during this quiet time. I assumed he was either praying or preparing a homily.

When we did chat my progress in school was a frequent query. "I taught Latin and English for a number of years," he informed me. Thankfully, he never quizzed me as might many teachers. Nor did he get religious and talk about Jesus and the saints or tell me I should pray for a vocation.

One day in the course of a discussion about the Boston Red Sox and Ted Williams, Father mentioned that as a kid he dreamed of being a baseball player. He pitched for his seminary team. "I had a good fast ball but couldn't throw a curve to save my soul." He smiled. "I think the Lord intervened. He needed priests more than pitchers."

Another afternoon I asked what made him decide to become a priest. His answer was brief and short on details, suggesting only that a generous God had blessed him with the gift of ministry. "It has been a wonderful life. I have been so fortunate." We had almost reached the green when he stopped and turned to me. "I have loved being a priest, I really have," he paused. "But I often wish I had someone to share the journey with me. It can be lonely at times." He said no more nor did I question him further. I handed him his putter and went to tend the flag.

At the end of the summer, with school set to start, Father gave me a holy card of St Joseph of Cupertino. Father informed me he was the patron saint of students. If the prayer on the card was faithfully recited before an examination, Father explained, the student would obtain the grace to be asked only questions to which he knew the answer. It apparently worked well for St. Joseph but not that great for me. Probably because I spent more time saying the prayer than studying.

My family moved back to the city for the winter, which took me out of the local news orbit; when we returned in the spring I learned that Father had died. To my surprise, he was only fifty-one years old. I felt bad and said a prayer for him next time I went to church. My family had a Mass said in his memory.

There have been times since when I have been on a golf course, in the shank of a glorious summer day, and remember the good Father and how he would enjoy such a scene. Then the thought occurs; perhaps he *is* watching from a celestial perch with a view infinitely better than mine.

10

A Pair of Generals

THE RECENT CONTROVERSY RELATED TO a statue of Gen. Robert E. Lee triggered a personal recollection. The incident involved another iconic military man: Erwin Rommel.

In 1963, on active duty with the U.S. Air Force, I used a week of leave for travel to Gargellen, a ski resort in the Austrian Alps.

Our military aircraft – a KC-135 – landed in Frankfurt. The distance to my destination necessitated an overnight stay at a former German – now American – military base at Boeblingen, in Germany's Garmisch-Partenkirchen region.

The dining room of the officer's club that Saturday night was filled with American military, many with their families. Those sitting at my table included three officers in uniform: a colonel, a major and a captain.

Midway through the meal there was a flurry of activity in the balcony. An older woman, perhaps in her seventies, and a younger, middle-aged man were being seated at a table. Their entrance was noticed by diners on the main floor, many of whom stood and applauded the couple who, in turn, acknowledged the welcome with smiles and a wave.

"Who are they?" I asked the Colonel.

He explained that it was Mrs. Rommel and her son Manfred. She had recently been ill and this – her first sighting in some weeks – made the welcome more spirited than usual.

As the meal progressed, I learned that during the war, Boeblingen was the primary facility for testing tanks and training crews. The base was Rommel's first command assignment: taking control, in 1940, of the 7th Panzer Division – which was one of the more storied German units during WWII.

Rommel had purchased a home about an hour from the base, to which he returned between military assignments. The family still maintained a residence there.

After dinner, I joined the captain, who was about my age (29) and of equal rank, at the bar for a nightcap. Jim, from Georgia, had a broad Southern accent, a good ol' boy personality and, beneath his well-tended uniform, beat – I soon learned - the heart of a rebel.

I expressed my surprise at the warm welcome given the Rommels and wondered if the greeting would be as friendly if the man himself had been present. I reminded Jim that Rommel was responsible for a lot of the crosses that line the American cemetery at Normandy.

Jim nodded and spoke of how Rommel seemed to have escaped it all, how he's remembered as an honorable man and a brilliant strategist who fought for his country, believed in the mission and supported his Fuhrer – until he didn't. "So, if he were here tonight I bet his welcome would be just as warm."

"Guess the situation is a lot like your Robert E. Lee," I said, "another general who fought the good fight and was admired on both sides of the line." I wondered whether if he walked into a Union officer's mess after the war, would they stand and applaud him.

Jim wasn't sure but felt he'd be shown respect and treated with courtesy – as Gen. Grant did at Appomattox.

Our friendly banter was not without the occasional jibe. I mentioned how misguided the thinking was which presumed a bunch of "hayseeds" could hope to defeat our Union boys. "Guess you crackers learned your lesson."

A grin accompanied Jim's disagreement. He acknowledged a couple of battle-field setbacks, but the surrender was, he claimed, a tactical ruse, a chance to regroup, to prepare for another day. His voice hinted of conspiracy. "Listen, my Yankee friend, the South will rise again. And one day, by God, Lee's statue will sit astride the Capitol Dome."

Jim raised his stein. "To General Lee." The toast accomplished, we declared a truce. The conversation turned to skiing.

The 2017 confrontation between those bent on the desecration of Lee's effigy and his stalwart defenders brought Jim to mind. Decades had passed since our meeting; time perhaps has sapped his vigor, but his allegiance, I'm certain, is as steadfast as it was the night we dined with the Rommels. His hope that the general's likeness would one day top the capitol's carapace appears less certain.

11

Caddy Days

MY FIRST EXPOSURE TO THE game of golf and the caddy experience occurred during the summer of 1946 when I was 12 years old. My family had a summer cottage on Point Judith Road, a leisurely twenty-minute walk from the Point Judith Country Club (PJCC). Whoever suggested that caddying would be a healthy, wholesome activity for a young boy to pursue saved me from summers of weeding a large vegetable garden, lawn-cutting, and an array of other boring chores that inevitably became my responsibility.

With the close of WWII, servicemen were slowly being discharged and returning to civilian life, but many positions formerly held by men remained unfilled. The caddy master at the PJCC, the man who assigned the bag-toting jobs, hadn't as yet been mustered out of the military.

This I learned one weekend morning in late June when I made my first appearance at the course. With no one making assignments, the dozen or so caddies, none of whom I knew, waited for golfers to arrive, then ran to greet them in the parking lot, and offered their services. This stampede did not favor the undersized novice. The golfers, as would be expected, more often chose the bigger boys and those who had carried for them in the past. On two occasions that day I actually had a bag on my shoulder – first time ever – and was set to take to the fairways when an older kid came along and pulled it away, muttering something to the effect I should go home.

In spite of my efforts over the first two days, I never acquired a job. The usual reason: golfer preference; the other: forcible insistence by a larger body. On the third day, my frustration continued. Serious thought was given to scratching my caddy ambitions. The only thing that held me back was the thought of the chores waiting at home.

Then my luck changed. The next morning I was again being separated from a bag when an older – early 20s – black man well over 6 feet tall said to the kid, "Let 'em have it." His voice was quiet but there was no mistaking its authority. Without hesitation, the boy released his grip on the bag and walked away. I had my first caddying job, a woman just learning to play the game. We were a perfect combination.

My benefactor was "Corny" Frye, one of three brothers who caddied at Point Judith. From that point on, having received his blessing, I gained equal footing with the others.

Sometime later I thanked Corny for what he had done that day. He laughed it off, then added, "You looked like a white boy who needed a break."

The next summer Arthur Diana, the caddy master, returned after his discharge from the military. Maintaining law and order within the caddy ranks took up a significant portion of his day. As judge and jury, Arthur meted out his punishments in proportion to the level of his aggravation. Freedom of speech and the right of appeal had not found their way into Art's court. The ultimate sentence was to be sent "up the road," that is home for a prescribed period. Usually the punishment was less dramatic: not being picked for a job over a day or two sent an equivalent message.

Now part of the group, I promptly learned to swear, smoke and survive in an occasionally hostile environment. Weekends in mid-summer, approximately 25 to 30 kids would be in attendance. The group was roughly split between white kids and colored kids, political correctness not a consideration at the time.

Waiting to be called for jobs, we spent the time rough-housing – occasionally leading to real fights – card playing and climbing into the rafters of the old polo barns rousting bats from their perches. A lean-to behind the pro shop provided shelter and a place to store lunches – which were invariably stolen – a dozen feet away was a classic two-holer with a stench that repelled all but the truly desperate.

Added to the questionable habits acquired that summer – smoking and bad language – was another: the taste of alcohol.

At that time, PJCC didn't provide a drink or snack shack on the course for the players who wished to enjoy a mid-round beverage. Players who felt the need for a pick-me-up would, after completing the 10th hole, send a caddy to the clubhouse to pick up the libations, his return coinciding with the player's arrival at the 13th tee. Those players absent a caddy carried their bags on the relatively short intervening holes. Almost always the drinks were of the alcoholic variety; a Tom Collins was a popular choice.

Occasionally I was tasked with this mission. The order filled, I made my way back to the course, glasses filled to the brim, crowded onto a tray. Spillage due to an uneven terrain was always a concern. That possibility, I reasoned, would be lessened if a sip or two were taken from glasses at particular risk. In this most innocent of circumstance I was introduced to the last of the bad habits available to me at the time – and one that has been maintained with some regularity since.

On days when business was slow, a few of us would stroll over to the tennis courts to watch the junior ladies cavort on the lush, grass courts. Between lessons and practice matches there were usually a half dozen or so available to ogle. Behind the screened back stop we watched as they darted about, bending and stretching in their white attire, tanned legs teasing beneath brief skirts. Our presence didn't seem to upset them; in fact, our comments of "good shot" often produced a smile. Eventually we'd be spotted, usually by a groundskeeper, and sent back "where you belong." Many of the tennis group also played golf; those adept at one sport, in most instances, seemed equally at ease with the other.

We all had our favorites: Glenna Vare – tall, blonde, tanned, with a face worthy of Hollywood – topped most lists, but four or five others with similar assets crowded second place. Our amorous intentions were guided by the experience, strategies and success of the more jaded of our number – the seventeen- and-eighteen-year-olds. But it was all talk. To my knowledge, no caddy had ever "made out" with a lady member -- with one exception.

Doug was from Wakefield, a junior in high school. For reasons even he couldn't explain, one of the females, a golfer – very attractive and of similar age – took a fancy to him.

With halting steps – as it was an awkward situation – their romance continued through the summer of 1948. Late afternoons were their time. She would request Doug as her caddy or arrange a meeting on the course.

Their favored rendezvous was a bush-crowded path through the woods, which led from the third green to the fourth tee. The advantage: before entering their hide-away, they could see any golfing activity on the first and second holes. Adjustments in the couple's activities were made accordingly.

Alas, their infatuation was not to last. The young lady's father somehow learned of his daughter's fascination with evening golf and her out-of-bounds activities and promptly took away her clubs for the remainder of the season. Doug continued to bask in the glow of conquest for the rest of the summer – and perhaps still does.

At sixteen I took a summer job – which continued through college – cutting fish at the Fisherman's Co-operative in Galilee. Other than Fridays, my caddy career was history.

In retrospect, to say that my experience at the country club provided a model of behavior that I could draw on later in life, the way men talk about their Eagle Scout experience or lessons learned while camping in the wilderness, would be a stretch. I did learn how to inhale without coughing, curse with conviction, appreciate the taste of liquor, and everything one needed to know about women, which – some years later – I found to be spectacularly bogus. On the business end I found that flattery and a little schmoozing work wonders in the tip area and became aware of an enviable stratum of society and that once in a while everyone needs a Corny Fry in their life.

12

The Day Romance
Invaded Block Island

IT IS LATE SEPTEMBER 1942 on Block Island, a modestly inhabited remnant of glacial retreat located off Rhode Island's south coast. Three people joined by war, weather, and the whimsy of a mischievous fate become the principals in an improbable tale of intrigue and romance.

Within weeks of America's declaration of war against Nazi Germany – December 11, 1941 – Hitler deploys submarine packs to the U.S. East Coast. Their mission: to prey on the convoys delivering military supplies and manpower to Europe. The initial success of the German U-boats is striking. A total of 348 ships are sunk during a four-months stretch in early 1942.

A factor that contributes to the dominance of the sub packs is data Germany obtains from informers strategically placed along the Eastern Seaboard. This loosely organized cadre consists primarily of German-trained agents brought by submarine to the United States and German-Americans sympathetic to the Axis cause. They pass on information (convoy size and speed, destroyer or aerial escort presence, weather conditions) to each other and the U-boat commanders lurking offshore.

During the early struggle for control of the shipping lanes, Germany's dominance is such that U-boats roam at will, apparently with little concern for detection. Fishermen report swastika-emblazoned subs lying at anchor off the eastern reaches of Long Island and the Elizabeth Island chain, south of Cape Cod. Townspeople of various coastal communities report young men, strangers to the local populace, who arrive in town to make a variety of purchases and then disappear. Though anecdotal, the observations are insistent enough to foster the possibility of German sailors in their midst.

A gray-haired man sits at a desk on the glass-enclosed deck projecting from the roof of his home. Since the death of his wife, the house on Block Island's southern coast, initially a summer retreat, has become a year-round residence. Perched on the crest of a modest hill surrounded by an acre of untended scrub brush, it reminds him of the cottage his family rented each summer at Cruxhaven, on Germany's North Sea coast. As a young boy growing up in the industrial haze and grime of Bremen, he vowed that one day he'd have a home on the ocean. Now, with the Atlantic at his doorstep, Walter Schrager is quite content to spend his remaining days on this untidy parcel of land.

His office desk is neatly kept: an official-appearing manual, resembling a phone book, to his left, a sheaf of paper-clipped documents before him. To his right, a leather binocular case. A nautical map of the East Coast of the United States spreads over one wall; a bulky shortwave radio sits atop a smaller table.

His presence this day is more indicative of habit than purpose: pillows of menacing clouds straddle the countryside, obscuring the magnificent panorama he typically enjoys. Finishing a cigarette, he lingers over coffee and moments later descends from his house-top aerie to a lower floor.

A short distance away, a young woman (also upset with the dismal weather), begins her day. Breakfast with her mother has become tedious, the conversations repetitive. Her mother is worried about her, asking time and again why she's so quiet, why the moodiness and bursts of temper, so unlike her. In fact, there's nothing wrong with Bobbi Hanley – she's nineteen and just plain bored.

Since high school graduation in June, her social life (parties and dances) has been nonexistent, as though the island is in quarantine. The war has taken all the cute boys, including Joey Kilmartin, the closest thing she had to a boyfriend during high school. A nice-looking guy and good athlete – captain of the football team. They had a few dates, one of which included her first and very unsatisfactory sexual experience. Although her mother likes him – he cut her lawn for free during the summer – he is just too full of himself, and Bobbi stopped returning his calls.

Most of her girlfriends have taken jobs on the mainland. For Bobbi, remaining on the Island, working in a marine-supply store and tending bar on the side isn't exactly the career path she had in mind. She has been offered a position in Providence beginning the first of the year but hesitates to leave her mother alone. The man of the house has been absent for more than a year.

After making her bed and tidying the room, Bobbi gives her mother a hug, and wrapped in a blue rain slicker, blonde hair ringing the hood, she bikes off to work.

A submarine is anchored about a mile offshore. A swastika painted on each side of the forward hull identifies its country of origin. Below deck, a young man stretches out on his bunk, one of six rigged in the cramped aft section, the least desirable location on the boat, reserved for first-time cruisers.

He has just returned from a meeting with the captain, who informed him that he will disembark the vessel that afternoon. A rubber dinghy is being readied. His assignment is to row ashore and obtain food supplies. A contact has provided the location of an easily accessible store.

Trips to shore, this being his second, make Hans anxious. Being the captain's choice has little to do with experience and more to do with his labored fluency in English. However, he gets along with the shipmate accompanying him: a gnarled older seaman hampered by injury who was chosen to allay suspicion.

Later, when the dinghy is ready, the pair – dressed in clothes lacking identification – push off from the sub and, in a choppy sea, row to a dim shoreline.

A thick fog sheaths Block Island's west coast, the residue of a fierce nor'easter that roiled the Atlantic waters during the previous week. The single-lane road that Bobbi takes to work follows the shoreline, skirting cliffs of crumbling limestone, past the smudged outline of the occasional dwelling. Further on, the cliffs recede, reduced to rock-strewn beaches studded with clusters of sturdy bushes and ragged, wind-swept dunes. Just before the breachway and the sprig of land that bends to the sea, an attentive traveler would notice three shingled structures set back from the road. Signs provide identification: Lem's Landing, General Store, and Marine Supplies – and two smaller buildings marked Showers and Beer/Ice. Behind the store, a dirt path lined by scrub pine leads to a small, crescent-shaped beach.

Inside the general store, Bobbi (pert and blonde, dressed in jeans, sneakers, and a floppy sweater) breaks down the shelves, stacking canned goods in crates scattered about the floor. Produce and perishable items will be placed in separate containers for disposal if not purchased before the close of operations in three days. Marine supplies occupy considerable space, identifying their primary customers: boaters (power and sail), who flock to the island during warmer months. The operation is seasonal, opening in May and closing in September.

Movement outside the window catches her eye. Two figures, shrouded in the mist, make their way along the path from the beach. Other than being late in the season, it isn't unusual when sea conditions worsen for boaters to anchor in the cove. Waiting out the foul weather, they often row to shore for beer and a real shower.

A knock on the door, a pause, and the pair cautiously enters. Dressed in black turtlenecks, trousers, rain slickers, and cloth caps, each has a duffel bag slung over his shoulders. One is considerably older and walks with a limp.

The young, taller one, seemingly in charge, asks in an accent, "Are you open to buy?"

"Closing soon," Bobbi replies, "but take your time." She grins. "Glad to get your business."

"We need groceries," the tall man says.

The older man smiles, shrugs his shoulders, and points to his mouth.

His companion explains, speaking slowly and without inflection, like someone who has learned English from books, "He understands English. Just can't speak it."

Somewhere from Europe, these two, Bobbi assumes. *Like we often get in the summer, one of those strange languages. But I have heard his accent somewhere before.*

Her attempts at small talk garner little response: their trip began "up north"; a "friend" suggested Block Island as refuge from the storm; their destination was "up to the captain."

Bobbi nods toward the shelves and the partially filled boxes. "Stocks are pretty low – end of the season."

The young man nods. "That is okay. Just something for a few days."

They bring their selections to the counter, mostly canned goods and what remains of the produce. Bobbi watches as they move about the store. They clearly aren't the usual boating clientele (ruddy-faced, garrulous types, delighted to recall their exploits at sea – real or imagined – and their plans for the next leg). She concludes the younger one, despite his pallor, shadowed cheeks, and deep-set, tired eyes, is cute. His quick food selections and frequent glances at his watch suggest a tenseness, unlike his gimpy-gaited companion, who pauses to read the labels on cans. An impish laugh punctuates his whispered asides to his more serious companion, some of which, Bobbi suspects, relate to her.

The counter is heaped with their provisions. The younger man turns to Bobbi.

"That will be good. We have plenty now. Thank you for your help." For the first time, he smiles.

At that moment two things happen: his face is erased of furrows and fatigue, and what Bobbi considered cute is now handsome.

Crisp American dollars settle their bill. They get ready to leave.

"You are very kind," says the now-handsome one. "What is your name?"

"Bobbi," she replies, smiling. "Roberta, actually, but everyone calls me Bobbi. And you?"

"Hans. My friend is Roscoe." After hesitating, and then glancing toward his partner, who returns a nod, he says, "I hope I am not rude"

– he stops momentarily – "but I think you are very pretty, Roberta." Their eyes lock, his gaze so intense she feels a shiver.

Bobbi feels her face flush. "You saved me some work. Next time you come through, stop in."

She takes a business card from the counter. She hesitates, then writes her phone number on the back of the card. "Here, take this, a reminder. You never know."

She watches from the side window as they walk down the path to the beach, bags slung over their shoulders, into the gloomy early evening.

The closing of Lem's General Store and Marine Supplies becomes official on a classic New England autumn day. The air is crisp and dry, the warming sun alone in the cloudless sky, a salt-scented breeze sweeping across the island. Bobbi secures the last of the window shutters when she sees a man approaching, his car parked at the side of the road. Introductions soon follow, and a badge pinned beneath his lapel identifies his official capacity: FBI.

The agent informs her that a German sub, operating off Block Island, was attacked by a Navy destroyer two nights before. In the debris that surfaced were cans of food that appear to have been bought locally.

"We don't feel the sub was destroyed, just stuff blown through the tubes to make us think so. We wondered if anything may have come from your store, and if you remember these guys."

Bobbi relates her story of the men in black. "I have no idea who they were, where they came from, or their destination – but one did have a familiar accent."

"Come with me, Miss; I'll show you some of the items."

A hodgepodge of refuse – bottles, clothing, vegetable cans, shreds of produce, blankets, and wadded paper items – fills the car trunk.

"Do you recognize anything, Miss?"

"Some things, like the food cans, are familiar, but any store would have the same. Nothing stands out."

"That's fine, Miss." After a few more questions, the agent thanks her. "If you think of anything else, please contact me." He hands her his card.

"So you really think the sub got away?" Bobbi asks.

The agent nods. "Probably. No oil slick, that's the giveaway. But I've got to say, they were a pretty nervy bunch, coming ashore like that. Or really hungry."

Hearing the sound of approaching aircraft, they both look up. A formation of Navy planes heads out to sea. As they approach the shore-line, sun reflects from a window below. *Probably Schrager's place*, Bobbi thinks. About to turn away, she remembers.

"Sir." Bobbi grabs the agent's arm. "The accent. I remember now. Mr. Schrager up on Beacon Hill." She points to the yellow house at the top of the hill. "The one with the glass deck."

"Who is he?" the agent asks.

"Old guy. Don't know much about him. Comes to the store for a newspaper once in a while. Nice man."

"You're sure he's the one with the same accent?"

"Positive."

The agent waves as he drives off. He doesn't take the road into town, but heads toward Beacon Hill.

Later, as she cycles home, the agent passes her, heading towards the ferry. Mr. Schrager sits in the passenger seat.

With her move to Providence the following January, Bobbi's social life improves. Training for a bank teller position exposes her to others in her age group, most with similar interests. Friday night's happy hour widens the circle. One Friday in the crowded bar, she hears her name shouted above the din. There's Joey Kilmartin, beer in hand, waving to her.

They chat. Home on leave, Joey has an appointment with a bank loan officer in the morning. When he gets out of the service, he's going into commercial fishing, and since he wants his own boat, he's getting the loan process started. *Sounds like the Army has grown this guy up,* she thinks. *The ambition of the Joey I remember didn't go beyond sneaking a few beers down to the beach on a Saturday night and hanging out with his buddies.*

Joey finishes his drink, apologizes for having to leave, is delighted to have bumped into her. He wonders if it would be all right to call when he gets home again. Bobbi smiles, tells him yes, and hopes he will be safe.

Bobbi, in fact, did enjoy their meeting, but it wasn't all related to Joey; it was just good to talk to someone from "the Block." To her surprise, Bobbi finds herself missing the place. The windswept desolation she once railed against has become more attractive. Not quite an epiphany, but she realizes that deep down she's a country girl, that the hustle and bustle of the city is not her style. This intuition hardens to conviction. Two cubicle-bound weeks later, she gives her notice to the bank and calls Lem. He'd be delighted to have her back when they reopen for the season.

Her decision to return home, she reasons, will ease her concerns about her mother's solitary existence. Although she knows it's more than that. Meeting Hans that dismal day last September and the undeniable flash of chemistry between them is a memory she can't dislodge. But harboring the notion that a man she met for mere moments, who offered only a compliment and electric blue eyes, would return to this godforsaken island – it's beyond ridiculous. When she tells her mother about him, her take is typically straightforward: "You've seen too many movies."

However, a determined Cupid isn't to be deterred, his sway transcending reason, logic, and all manner of mortal upheaval. As the story goes, in the summer of 1946, the most improbable of pairings comes to pass. On a brilliant late-August evening, Bobbi's sailor walks off the Block Island ferry, finds a telephone kiosk, and calls a number written on the small card fished from his wallet.

When Bobbi informs her mother of Hans's arrival, the conversation does not go well. Her first reaction is shock, the second is trying to catch the coffee cup she was drying before it fell to the floor. What she thought was little more than a figment of her daughter's romantic imagination has become a reality.

"Wait until you meet Hans, Mom, you'll really like him. We can have him for dinner some night."

The look she gave Bobbi does not register hospitality. "I don't want to meet this man and I certainly don't want him in my house. If your father were here, he'd throw him off the island. Feed him? I'd like to poison him. He's a goddam Nazi, Bobbi."

"The war's over, Mom."

"The war may be over but I'm not about to love my enemy just yet. Apparently you are."

"I do feel guilty for liking him but can't help it. He doesn't hate Americans. He was just a sailor who did what he was ordered to do - which was to join ..."

"... and blow up unarmed American tankers right off our coast here. You've seen the oil on the beaches. Thousands of men are at the bottom of the Atlantic because of bastards like him. Traipsing around here like he's a tourist while old man Schrager who never hurt anyone in his life sits in a jail cell."

"I'm sorry about all that, Mom. Especially Mr. Schrager. I was just trying to be helpful. But that's got nothing to do with Hans. You're making him sound like a bad person. And he's not."

"I'm calling him a willing accomplice. And I'm calling you a traitor."

Bobbi begins to cry. "Okay, I won't bring him by, Mom. But I'm going to see him when I want."

"Maybe he'll take you back to Germany with him. Maybe he has a castle. Live happily ever after. Like in Hollywood."

"I'm going to stay with him tonight."

"Go."

"I'll sweep up the glass before I leave."

"I said, *go*."

Over the next two weeks the couple – judged by the locals to be an attractive pair – are frequently seen about the island, walking the beaches hand in hand, dancing at the Ballard's resort, dining at the Atlantic House, an idyllic interlude for a couple seemingly taken with each other.

But news travels quickly around a small town. And Bobbi senses a coolness, an aloofness, when she and Hans strike up conversations with storekeepers, sales people and even bartenders as though it is somehow unpatriotic for them to be cordial to an old enemy.

Her hope that Hans would not pick up on the rudeness is dashed one afternoon as they walk through town. A couple of boys – high school kids – begin shouting from across the street, "Go home, Kraut."

Hans waves off her apologies. "I'm not surprised. A natural reaction. It happened in German too. I hated the Americans. I was told to. It didn't last long. Very fast they started rebuilding the bombed-out cities. Like Hamburg where I'm from, everything is new, trains, subways, skyscrapers. Now they love the Yanks. People forget after a while."

Bobbi tells him about the scene with her mother. "I really wanted you to meet her. She's a very kind, gentle person most of the time. Except when she erupts. I haven't heard her swear since my father was around."

"Maybe next time she'll be better."

"I wouldn't plan on it. But at least she's talking to me again."

An excellent sailor, Hans suggests – for his last weekend – they rent a sailboat for a day sail to Cuttyhunk a small island in the waters south of Cape Cod. Bobbi agrees and on a flawless September day, with a breeze ideal for long tacks and a half-dozen cans of beer, they set sail. Approaching the island's anchorage, Hans mentions that the place has hardly changed from his last visit.

"You've been here before? When?

"I'll tell you. You'll enjoy it." After a long sip of beer Hans begins. "The day before I met you at the store our sub surfaced not too far from where we are right now. We needed to recharge the ship's batteries and for me and Roscoe to go ashore for food. We circled the island, but the captain couldn't find a stretch of beach where we could land our dinghy. The entire coastline was lined with big rocks. The captain wouldn't take the chance. He decided to go to Block Island instead. The rest you know. And, here we are. In the same waters. Back where it began."

"What a great story, Hans. How close we came to not meeting."

"Maybe fate meant us to be with each other, Bobbi. What do you think?" Hans is grinning as he asks the question but there is a hint of seriousness in his tone.

Bobbi smiles and shrugs her shoulders.

The man Bobbi sees before her – relaxed, enjoying the sun-filled summer day has changed. An improved English fluency has widened their conversations and uncovered his sense of humor. Still a young man, he talks of the brave ideas he has for his future. Like his father, he wants to be a banker. But no longer is he the handsome man of Bobbi's dreams. The intense, blue eyes remain but the sharp, sculpted facial features are soft and indistinct, his hair – gray at the temples – has retreated to mid-scalp. The lean, lithe body has acquired a paunch. Nor has the chemistry of their first meeting returned. Nor would it. The certainty of that intuition was realized one evening in the middle of a goodnight kiss. In the twinkle of an eye whatever romantic feelings she had for Hans disappears. The sadness that later disturbs her sleep has cleared by morning, replaced by a sense of relief.

The morning of Hans' departure, the Island residents are preparing for the arrival of a storm that is approaching hurricane status. Already sheets of rain have begun their assault, pelting the roof of Bobbi's VW bug as they make their way through the deserted countryside to town and the ferry pier.

"What a barren place this is, Bobbi, especially when the weather turns bad. Wonder how people stand it through the winter."

"You get used to it. For me no matter how wild and desolate it gets, there's still a beauty about the place. A harsh beauty maybe but whatever it is suits me."

"Visit with me in Germany. I would love to show you my country."

Bobbi shrugs her shoulders. "That's something I've always wanted to do. But right now, Hans, I can't leave my mother. She's not doing that great. She needs me."

"I understand." He pauses, his voice hesitant. "Tell me, Bobbi. Was it a mistake for me to come back? Maybe I should have left it alone? But I had to see you again."

"And it was the same for me. So, I think it's good that you did come back. We needed to find out and not be forever pining for each other, wondering what might have been. We've had a good time together and now we are friends." She pointed ahead; the town had come into view. "The ferry's in and it looks like they're loading."

At the dock, the boat crew positions cars on the lower deck. The boat lanyards roped to the wharf groan with the bursts of wind. Beyond the harbor the bay is studded with white caps. A dockside sign indicates this to be the last trip to the mainland today.

Hans leans toward Bobbi. His lips lightly graze her cheek. "Thank you. I had a wonderful time."

"I enjoyed it too. Hope you have a safe trip."

"Thanks, take care."

Then he is gone, a misted figure hunched into the wind. She puts the windshield wipers on for a last look. Her eyes – which she thought would be overflowing with tears at this moment – remain dry. At the gangplank Hans turns, gives a short wave and boards the ferry.

Bobbi doesn't stay to watch the ship leave. Departing the parking lot, she dials in a music station and heads toward home. *A cup of coffee with my mother sounds awfully good about now. I can tell her how this movie ends.*

On the front page of the February 10, 1948, morning edition of the *Providence Journal,* the following story appears:

SUSPECTED SPY RELEASED

After six years in Federal Custody and home confinement, 77-year-old Walter Schrager, a suspected German spy during WWII, has been released. A resident of Block Island, Mr. Schrager was arrested in September 1942, and charged with conducting espionage for the Germans. After numerous appeals filed by his lawyer, it was determined by a federal judge in New York that the evidence presented by the government was insufficient, the case being driven more by bias than documentation.

The same year, the June 10th edition of the *Narragansett Times,* in its "Block Island Happenings" column, offers the following:

This past Saturday, Saint James Catholic
Church was the scene of a wedding celebration. Joined in matrimony by Father Kelnew
were Roberta Hanley and Joseph Kilmartin.
Both are Block Island natives and will
reside on the island after a wedding trip
to Cape Cod. Joan Golden was the maid of
honor; best man, Thomas Kilmartin.

Author's note: The basic elements of this story were supplied by Captain "Dub" Barrows, a retired commercial fisherman with whom I worked at the Point Judith Fisherman's Co-Operative in Galilee, RI.

13

A MEETING IN CAPE TOWN

DAVID HURRIES THROUGH THE still-considerable throng at dockside, his eyes fixed forward, hoping to avoid prolonged good-byes or nostalgic post-voyage conversations. A few blocks later, safely immersed in the anonymous crowds of Cape Town, he hails a taxi.

"Yes, sir," the black driver tells him. "Know the Colonial well. 'Bout a half-hour." His smile, enriched by a gold tooth, fills the rearview mirror.

With this assurance David removes his jacket and settles himself into a cramped back seat. A few insistent hand signals and muttered oaths later, the driver eases the cab into the crush of vehicles. Traffic lights, it becomes apparent, are but options for the drivers to consider; policemen at the larger intersections, their arms flailing, are equally ignored. Clusters of people mill about a series of sidewalk vendors, steam rises from their large gray pots, meat roasts on charcoal grills and aromas of spice and smoke spill into the cab. Down a side street, a group of women outfitted in multicolored costumes and clutching placards – on which are written bible verses - are singing with evangelical fervor A small boy blowing on a trumpet stands off to the side.

The "half-hour" passed fifteen minutes earlier. Beyond the city center, the streets are less obstructed, and pedestrians proceed unimpeded, the driver finally able to move beyond first gear.

"Getting closer, Mister?" David asks the driver, his tone more curious than one of concern. That the planned afternoon tryst might be unwise had been briefly considered but discarded. For David, randy expectation had always trumped caution – occasionally to his chagrin.

The driver doesn't answer, but gestures ahead.

A small park with a scattering of wooden benches and half a dozen gaunt, brown-leafed trees sits across from a block of buildings. From the center of the group a red brick structure protrudes. A tattered green canopy extends from its broad wooden door to the curb. A pair of impressive wrought-iron light fixtures, perhaps suggesting a more elegant time, flank the entrance. The sign hanging by cables from the brow of the building announces in colored lights: *The Colonial Hotel.*

The cab circles the park to its opposite side. A single black car is parked just beyond the hotel. Otherwise the street is empty, as is the park, except for two couples chatting across a broad stone table.

David looks at his watch. *Getting close,* he thinks, *but she said she'd wait until three. He shakes his head. Two weeks ago who'd have thought we'd end up here – a beat-up hotel in a forgotten part of town? And it started so innocently…*

On an overcast December afternoon a cruise ship departs Tenerife in the Canary Islands, embarking on a two-week voyage along Africa's west coast to Cape Town, South Africa. As the ship dips through the choppy waters of Porto Grande Bay, a crowd gathers on the aft deck to watch and photograph the departure.

Among the group leaning over the rail, his hands cradling a gin and tonic, is David Greene. Nothing about his appearance could be considered striking. Though of middle age (53) and grazing six feet, his slimness fosters the impression of a taller man; the abundance of blond hair, hinting of gray at the temples, a younger one. Acquaintances, of which he has many, often remark on this fortunate disparity. Good friends, of whom he has few, aren't as impressed.

David finishes his drink. As he considers another, he feels a tap on his shoulder.

He turns to see a woman in a bright blue windbreaker with eyes to match. "Excuse me," she says to him, "but if I could get to the rail for a picture, please?" She has an accent, and a smile that denies refusal. Fine lines about her eyes suggest mileage; the tilt of her head, mischief. A circle of blonde hair rings the hood of her jacket.

David nods. "Sure," he answers. "Get in here. Take your time."

After adjusting the camera's lens with apparent familiarity, she snaps a series of photos. In the process, a large diamond on her marital finger glitters into view.

She turns to leave. "Thanks again."

"Shall I take one of you?" David asks. "Looks like a pretty complicated camera. Just show me what to push."

"Oh, that would be nice," she replies. After some adjustments, she hands him the camera and indicates the operative button. Her perfume – a light, playful fragrance with a hint of jasmine – suits well the casual moment.

She tugs back her hood. Blonde hair spills to her shoulders. With a dazzling smile in place she extends her arms along the rail, and David takes about half a dozen shots of her from different angles.

He hands back the camera, adding a smile to the exchange. "Hope I got your best side."

Her lips form to reply, but lapse instead to a grin. David watches as she crosses the deck.

David reclaims his rail position. Clouds are scudding to the east, opening windows of auburn skies in their wake. Persistent gulls dip and glide in the ship's draft, the more cautious having retreated to port.

He glances at his watch. Guess it's time to go to work.

Most of the passengers on this medium-sized ship can be accommodated on the open area of the middle deck. There they have gathered in response to an invitation to meet the folks who will be providing their services during the cruise. The introductions are handled by the cruise director, an energetic English chap with whom David has sailed before. Multi-talented, the director was trained as a classical pianist but, citing economic necessity, worked the vaudeville circuit in England as a singer/comedian before joining the cruise industry.

In no particular order, representatives of various departments come forward and offer brief remarks about their backgrounds and their roles during the voyage. In due course, the cruise director introduces David, who takes his position on a makeshift podium at the corner of the pool and begins:

"Good afternoon, everyone. I'm David Greene. With this accent you can undoubtedly surmise I'm from the United States. I, along with my colleague Fritz – whom I've just met – are the gentlemen hosts for this cruise. It is our pleasant task to socialize with passengers traveling alone – specifically the single ladies.

"We are available for dancing in the bar before and after dinner and in the lounge on the upper deck until the wee hours. Please, if you're at all inclined, even if it has been years, we are here to make that happen.

"I recognize some passengers from previous trips and look forward to visiting with them, and to meeting all of you during the course of what I'm sure will be a splendid trip. Now, please welcome Fritz, the other half of the team."

During the course of his remarks, Fritz notes this is his first cruise as a gentleman host. David is reminded that he is beginning his tenth voyage. He remembers the first – Barcelona to Barbados. Shipboard routine and duties have scarcely changed, their repetition often tedious. For David, however, the excitement and anticipation felt on his maiden voyage has endured, the allure of "faraway places with their strange-soundings names" as palpable now as it was those years ago.

Starting back to the cabin after the introductions, David hears his name called. A man standing at the bar beckons. From a distance the man appears to be in his late 40s, taller than David, with a shaved, glistening scalp. A white, collarless, buttoned shirt stretches tautly across the man's chest. His informal dress and casual manner suggest he's from the States.

"Hi," he says, extending his right hand to David, "I'm Tom." A tattoo adorns his opposite forearm. "I must say, I'm intrigued by your job. Never heard of you guys before. Regular gigolos."

"We hear that all the time," David replies, smiling. "Not all that exciting, believe me. Wish it were. Most of the ladies are widows who like to travel, like having someone to talk with, dance with, have dinner with, things like that. They're comfortable with us. They know the cruise line checks us out pretty well. Some women won't take a cruise unless guys like us are on board."

Tom leans toward him, a smirk on his face. "Yeah, that's the party line, but I bet a lot of hanky-panky goes on. I imagine some of these rich old broads would pay good for a little tingle." His voice lowers to a good-ol'-boy, man-to-man register. "C'mon, David, off the record."

Whatever does go on, David thinks, *it's none of this guy's business.* Sure, stuff has been known to happen: the single lady's cabin door that quietly opens and closes during the night – and does again sometime later; the wife who encourages her husband's after-dinner drinking and sleep medication, facilitating a stroll after midnight; the cruise director who, having been approached by a generous lady, suggests to a gentleman host that he visit with her. *But this guy sure'n hell doesn't need to know.*

"Yeah," he replies. "After the trip some gents have gotten together with passengers. But any intimacies on board, you're hustled off at the next port." David is struck by the intensity of this guy's gaze – his eyes, though brown and friendly, never waver, hardly blink. *Is the guy gay*, he wonders. *Not the usual type but you never know.*

Time to change chat direction, David decides. "Noticed your tattoo, Tom," he tells him. "Can't quite make it out."

Tom raises his left arm to display the Marine Corps symbol with *Semper Fi* scrolled in a calligraphy style beneath it. *Well, that eases the gay concerns*, David assumes. "Any combat, Tom?"

"Yeah, lots. Iraq a couple of times."

"How'd that go?"

"Except for one bad day, okay."

"What happened?" *Keep it short, please*, he thinks. *God bless them, but some of these guys go on forever when they get started on the war.*

"Not much to tell," Tom says. "On patrol outside Mosul with my usual crew. Hit a land mine. Blew the Humvee to hell. Killed my buddy and almost two others. I got out with singed hair and a few burns." He runs his hand over his scalp and smiles. "Had some then. Just one problem."

"What's that?"

"Guess you haven't noticed." He signals the barman for a drink and lights a cigarette. "I'm deaf. The explosion blew out my drums. All kinds of surgeries didn't help."

Dave shakes his head. "My God, Tom, but we've been talking and…"

"I'm okay with men's voices a short distance away. But," he adds, "I've compensated. I read lips, and I've gotten very good at it."

Well, David thinks, *that explains the laser gaze.* "So what are you doing now?"

Tom hesitates momentarily. "Work in the insurance business mostly, as a subcontractor. If there are concerns about a claim, we – I've a lady partner – check it out. Also some private stuff. We've got a good reputation, and if someone needs some help, they call us. Out of Europe, mostly."

"What brings you on this trip?"

"Never cruised before. Got a pretty good deal so thought I'd try it."

David glances at his watch. "Look, I've got to push on, Tom. Fritz and I are meeting the single ladies at six. We'll chat again."

"Off you go," Tom says with a smile. "I'm going to keep my eye on you two guys. Might sign up myself one of these days."

"Sure. Why not? Can always use one of those few good men."

The announcement of a singles get-together in the lounge elicits a meager response, as it often does when scheduled for the first evening. Unpacking, jet lag, and fatigue are the very reasonable excuses. Of the six ladies who appear, four are widowed, and the remaining pair are younger and traveling separately. Curiosity regarding gentlemen hosts seems to be their primary conversational interest:

"Do you have a job in the real world?"

"Have a wife or girlfriend at home?"

"What do they think of all this socializing with the ladies?"

"How much do you get paid?"

In response to the last (frequently asked) query, David will occasionally answer that hosts are paid by the dance, like piecework. "You remember ten cents a dance?" he will say. "Well, we get two dollars. All tallied in a little book we carry." At some point during the trip the ladies learn otherwise, and, if they are good sports, enjoy the joke.

After a pleasant meal, the suggestion to the ladies of an after-dinner drink, and perhaps a dance in the bar, is rejected. Pleading fatigue, they suggest another time.

The turbulent waters of the early evening have eased. A full moon, framed in a spray-stained window, lightens the sea's face. Over a beer in an empty lounge, excepting Mario at the keyboard, David learns something of his roommate.

Fritz, born in Germany, speaks fluent, lightly accented English. Gray-flecked hair and a craggy face suggest an age of late 50s or early 60s. Within three months of earning his engineering degree from the University of Berlin he received a job offer from a fledging computer outfit in the United States. He accepted the offer and became one of Hewlett-Packard's first fifty employees.

"That worked out well," David says. "What prompted that fortunate choice?"

"Total luck," Fritz replies. "I had received offers from other companies in the U.S., but I was dead broke. They were the only one who would pay my airfare from Europe. It was a great company to work for. I had a great run. Retired six months ago, after twenty-four years."

David's hint at the probability of a well-endowed retirement package returns a nod and a half-smile. As to what prompted his gentleman host role, Fritz says he is unattached and likes to dance and travel. Also, since his wife's death a year earlier, he hasn't met a woman with whom he would care to spend two weeks.

"Well," David suggests with a smile, "your luck may change on this cruise. Your next romance may be but a deck away as we speak. Women enjoy a good dancer, and an accent goes a long way. And if you need some alone time down the road, I can make myself scarce."

"Don't think that's going to happen," Fritz answers, smiling. "Plus, I've read the rules for us guys. They come down pretty hard on that type of thing."

They chat a while longer. David's impression: a bright, friendly guy with a good sense of humor, which augurs well for their co-habitation over the next two weeks. Unfortunately, he appears burdened with an excess of scruple.

The following morning, between the fruit juices and cereals in the breakfast buffet line, David meets his camera-lady. While they assemble items on their trays, he learns her name, Inga, her nationality, German; and that she is traveling with her husband, Otto. As she heads back to join him, she turns to smile.

Choosing a table strategically situated allows David a more careful assessment of the physical package. Her height, blonde hair, blue eyes, and hints of aging are remembered from the previous afternoon. What this day reveals, as she visits at a nearby table, is a body that in another time would be described as voluptuous. She wears her height well: erect carriage, shoulders back and square, purposeful of stride. From ample breasts to compact chassis, her body gives a sense of solidity. He can imagine her during her teen years – one of those Aryan beauties Leni Riefenstahl sought to photograph and Hitler to propagate. She reminds David of women he has seen in Swiss and Austrian ski lodges: bodies to die for, but faces often tattered by sun, wind, and time. Inga has a way to go, but her last runs are on the horizon.

Otto appears to be in his mid-to-late seventies. Abundant gray hair, a full, florid face, jowls that gently lap his collar, and a complementary girth project the image of the prosperous businessman.

Passing through the lounge later in the day, David hears a voice call out, "Hello, young man!" He turns. An elderly lady is waving at him from a corner table, a newspaper spread before her and a pack of cigarettes, a box of matches, and a teacup set off to the side. He approaches her table.

"At least you can say hello," she begins. "I'm a single woman. Aren't you fellows supposed to look out for people like me?" She extends her hand. "I'm Margaret."

Her grip is firm, the palm rougher than he would have expected. "I didn't see you tucked away over here, Margaret," he says. "Very glad to meet you. I'm David."

They chat. David's contribution consists of nods and smiles at appropriate intervals. She cruises frequently, she says, but this is her first experience on this line. He listens with polite attention as she recalls her travel experiences. During the course of the conversation, David notices she's wearing a pair of bright red sneakers.

David assumes she is one of a subset of passengers he has encountered on other trips: elderly ladies with the financial resources to maintain, for extended periods, a shipboard residence, some leaving only for holidays or significant family events. Their rationale: here they are treated as royalty – the crew at their beck and call, the finest of accommodations, gourmet dining, top-notch medical availability, and a revolving door of new and interesting people. Not for these ladies the imagined nursing-home scenario: pungent, claustrophobic cells, gray walls festooned with stained photos and Kincaid prints, the ceaseless TV flicker, abysmal food, and – viewed through the single, locked window – the advertised pastoral scene: a square of unfortunate flowers cowering in a tangle of weeds.

The chat ends with Margaret admitting she is an incorrigible gossip. She encourages David to share with her any juicy morsels that may come his way. "At my age," she says, "that's all I have left." He promises to visit regularly. As she reaches for her cigarettes, he notes the Gauloises brand and mentions their reputation as one of the strongest cigarettes available.

"Did you know, Margaret," he asks, "some restaurants in France, where they're popular, won't allow them because of the smell they give off?"

She nods, but answers that when she smokes she wants the real thing, like Camels in the States. David would like to tell her what Camels did to his father, but he's certain it would make little difference.

Thinking about their meeting later, David feels a disconnection. The trappings of an elderly woman – straight gray hair, granny glasses, a loose, mousy dress, no jewelry or makeup, a cane by her side – are evident. But the bright, curious eyes, the snappy rejoinders, the firm, tight neck, an unlined face, the perfect teeth are at odds with the presentation. A young girl dressed in her mother's clothes comes to mind. With minimal intervention – hair-rinse and styling, ditch the glasses, a dress with some flair, earrings, necklace, lipstick – she would be an attractive, younger-appearing woman. *Perhaps*, David thinks, *the whole appearance thing is contrived. But that makes no sense. Why would someone take a two-week cruise and not wish to be recognized?*

The captain's welcoming reception, a formal event, is held in the theater on the second night of the cruise. Elegantly coiffed ladies splendid in their gowns and gentlemen handsomely outfitted in tuxedos enjoy drinks, hors d'oeuvres, and the band's offerings as they await the captain's entrance. This, the first social occasion when all passengers are together in one place, transforms what have been nods and smiles into introductions and ice-breaking badinage. The role of gentlemen hosts on this occasion is to mingle and socialize, alert to unaccompanied ladies who wish to dance or chat over a drink.

Inga and her husband arrive. She is fashionable in her ivory-colored, sequined gown. Otto has his arm around her waist. They make their way to a circle of three couples, who greet them with an easy familiarity. They are part of the German/Swiss contingent on board – nationalities always well represented on this line.

Although Otto is obviously older than she, they are a handsome couple, the type one sees – in suitably elegant surroundings – adorning travel brochures. As David watches their interactions, he suspects this is not Otto's first marriage, and probably not Inga's. For someone his age, it appears he has made an appropriate choice: an attractive woman, socially adept, sedately garbed – restrained glitz and décolletage – nicely situated between clueless bimbo and dotty matron. The frequent smiles and glances they share, their whispered asides, point to an easy rapport.

Maybe, David thinks, *I have misread her signals, and she's simply a friendly person.* But in similar scenarios in the past his intuition has been spot-on, and he still trusts it. Beneath that stylishly muted facade, he's convinced, lies a vixen.

By the time the captain and the ship's officers appear, passengers are scattered about the theater, pocketed in conversation, the comfortable hum of their chatter pervading the space. Others dance on the stage. The strangers of a short time ago are becoming neighbors.

During the next two days, they cruise the Cape Verde archipelago, a series of islands, volcanic in origin, lying about five hundred miles off the African coast. Their location provided replenishment of provisions and a safe haven for the original Portuguese and Spanish explorers en route to the Americas and India. The verdant topography that inspired the name of the archipelago is no longer, for the vast tracks of forest were decimated by shipbuilders during the 1500's.

Senegal is the first stop on the African continent. The capital, Dakar, was – as explained by the guide – the major embarkation port for slaves from West Africa to the West Indies and America. Awaiting the ship's arrival, they were held in segregated buildings on Goree Island, clearly visible from shore. An interesting criterion was used in the purchase arrangement: a slave – either male and female – had to weigh 140 pounds or more. The rationale was twofold: size equated with strength for work, and the odds of survival favored a larger person who was less likely to succumb to the primary cause of death on the voyage: dehydration.

Banjul, Gambia is our next port of call. Our visit is necessarily brief as the natives are not friendly and, in some instances, openly hostile. Groups of boys wandering the crowded, debris-strewn streets shout insults at the "foreigners" and, in some instances, surround them and demand money. Our guide, a young Gambian girl, eventually calls for a van that takes us back to the ship.

Settling into shipboard life, passengers heretofore anonymous are starting to surface. Couples and single ladies who previously remained in their rooms or strolled the deck before dinner now venture into the bar for a drink. The dining room schedule is reasonably flexible, allowing a very adequate happy hour – or two – for socialization and dancing.

As a result, David and Fritz are busy "working the room." A frequent scenario involves ladies who wish to dance but whose escorts are less than enthusiastic. Easily recognized, they are usually sitting near the dance floor, their feet tapping and torso moving in time to the music. Permission to dance with the gentleman's lady is usually granted, often with a measure of gratitude. A similar scenario prompts David, encouraged by a glance or two from Inga, to approach her husband. His nod of permission allows a few turns around the floor with his wife. The arm's length separation she maintains narrows appreciably when beyond the range of her husband's gaze.

The dining room, at the evening sitting, provides the ideal setting for becoming acquainted with your shipmates. Multiple nationalities comprise the manifest, most of whom are well traveled and successful in a variety of endeavors. An imaginative menu and excellent wine list encourages conversation, which, though occasionally pedantic, is always informative, unfailingly humorous, and frequently fascinating. David cannot recall an itinerary where the variety of discourse – abetted by the open seating format – has not been a highlight of the cruise.

He remembers one evening when, totally by chance, his table included a Battle of Britain Spitfire pilot, a German Messerschmitt pilot and an Oxford English professor who had chronicled Churchill's role in World War II. The German airman had a moderate cognitive impairment, and, as a result, was socially withdrawn.

"Where was he stationed?" asked the professor.

"Landstuhl," the airman's wife answered, "for most of the war. Do you know it?"

Before he could answer, the English airman chimed in. "I know it well, unfortunately. I flew spitfires out of Biggin Hill and we ran up against those buggers all the time. Tough lot they were."

"What did he fly?"

About to respond, his wife was interrupted. "Messerschmitt 109." It was the voice of her husband. "A great plane."

We all turned. His appearance seemed changed. No longer slouched in his chair, his eyes bright, face animated, he blossomed before us.

Although his short-term memory was shattered, he clearly recollected details of his war years: fellow fliers, number of kills (five), and even the tail number of his last aircraft. The back-and-forth between the pilots and the professor was magical, as was the evening, which lasted well beyond the Port, grapes, and Stilton cheese. His wife was absolutely astounded.

Swinging away from the African coast, the ship begins a four-day stretch at sea – an interval welcomed by some, resigned to by others. Accordingly, two categories of cruise passenger can be broadly identified.

First are those who enjoy frequent landfalls and are eager to interact with the local populace, share their history, and explore their culture. For them, the dull facade of a limitless ocean for days on end is a colossal bore.

At the other end of the spectrum are those who, if they never saw land, would be perfectly happy. Stretched on a deck chair, warming under the sun, watching an array of colors roil the sea's face, catching up on books long held in abeyance, they – perhaps with a glass of chilled Riesling at hand – enjoy leisurely discussions on subjects of scant importance with like-minded passengers. This, in their minds, is time well spent.

The itinerary of this cruise satisfies both preferences. Half of the voyage is spent at sea, the remaining days in port with a variety of land excursions available.

On sea days, educational lectures relevant to the upcoming landfall are presented each morning in the theater. A variety of other topics – e.g., wine tasting, food demonstrations – the local art – are interspersed through the schedule.

Dance lessons are conducted, with instruction provided by the principal dancers in the ship's entertainment group. If they are not available, then the gentlemen hosts assume the role. On this voyage, a Polish couple with multiple European dance championships in their resume give the lessons. The class includes four couples, two single ladies, and Inga. David watches as she moves about the floor. In the simplest of outfits – form-fitting khaki pants, a white blouse loosely gathered at the waist, and a circle of green scarf – she is striking.

After class they chat over soft drinks. David learns of their centuries-old home a short distance from Zürich, used by German diplomats during World War II; her passion for skiing; her two sons in college; and the fulfillment she has found in her work as a psychologist. Her English at times confuses tenses and jumbles syntax, but her accent, rather than a distraction, brings a cosmopolitan flair and a hint of intrigue to the exchange.

"Sounds like an interesting life," David says. "I'd like to hear more."

"You will, but not today," she replies with a hint of urgency. "I must go." As she turns, her hand pauses briefly on his. Then she walks quickly away. David watches her in the bar mirror as she hurries down the corridor. Beyond her is a large man with a white shirt and gray hair, who, although a good distance away, looks like Otto.

Leaving the theater after a lecture the next afternoon, David sees Inga sitting in one of the back rows. She waves. He joins her. "Visit with me for a while," she tells him as she nods toward a seat next to her. "Sorry I left so quickly yesterday."

"Your husband was looking for you?"

"Yes, but in the afternoon now he naps. So we can talk more." She smiles. "I fill in some details from yesterday."

There, in the semi-darkness of the empty theater, her story unfolds. Married at eighteen, she remained so for twenty years. The last years proved difficult, with infidelities on both sides. With their boys in secondary school, soon on their own, the couple mutually agreed to divorce. Her husband left, and neither she nor the boys has seen or heard from him since.

"It must have been a difficult time," David says.

"It was a terrible time. Not only no money, but more important, the boys losing a father they adored. An awful, cruel thing he did to them."

"And then Otto came along. How did you meet?"

"A long story, so I speak quickly." She glances at her watch. "I was working as a secretary to the boss of a chemical company. A man who was looking to buy the company would say hello whenever he came by. Old man – I had no interest. After a month about he asks me to go out for a drink. So why not, I think to myself. We meet at a nice bar and we talk. Small things like politics and business. Then dinner. He is very intelligent and knowledgeable in many things. I am also curious, so I enjoyed the time. We had several such dates. Very courteous, no suggestions. You know what I mean, David?"

"Not a dirty old man?"

"No, he was always very respectful. And me just a secretary. Anyway, one night having an after-dinner drink, he said he has a proposition for me. 'Okay,' I say, 'what?' He begins by telling me his age, his physical problems, and that he couldn't have sex anymore. He went on a bit longer. Then, like a shock of lightning, he asks me to marry him. I am dumbstruck. He sees this, and raises his hand and asks me to hear him out. Since his wife died, he said, eight years before, he lacks a woman to be with him on social occasions, to travel with, to talk with. I was the first person he felt comfort with in many years."

"Were you dating anyone at the time?"

"Yes, once in a while. But bringing up two boys, working, going to school three nights a week. No serious relationship. Anyway, most important, this man said he would give money for college for my boys. Also, no more work for me, full study at the university, and a good allowance. And, in return, my companionship and be faithful."

"Not a bad deal. You'd be set for life. So what did you do?"

"Okay, I talk to my boys. They would go with anything I wanted. My life was going nowhere. I'm getting older. A chance like this I'll never get again. So after much thinking, and even prayers, after a month I said yes to him. We got married."

"That's a helluva story. But you're a healthy woman. What about the sex part?"

"I have a friend from the old days. We are very careful. When Otto is away, I take train to Zurich and then taxi to a hotel. There we get together." She pauses. "So that's my story. I must go." She stands and blows a kiss in his direction. "See you at dance in the morning."

As she reaches the heavy curtains at the theater entrance, she stops and turns. "Funny about my friend," she says. "I called him twice before I left. Never got back to me." She shakes her head as if puzzled, then a quick wave, and she's gone.

Heading back to the cabin, David sees Margaret in her usual perch in the lounge, her accoutrements – computer, books, pack of Gauloises, box of wooden matches, cup of tea – all in place. David stops to chat. She offers her impressions of the ship thus far: food – "exquisite," wine selections – "fair," fellow travelers – "undecided," the captain – "a flirt." Then, without breaking stride, she asks, "How are you making out with the blonde?"

"What blonde?"

"Oh, David, don't be coy with an old lady. I saw you dancing the other night. There wasn't much daylight between the two of you."

David laughs. "Are you spying on me? I'm just doing my job."

"Okay, David." She wags her finger at him. "Don't do it too well. She has a husband, you know."

"I do know, Margaret. But thanks for the warning."

Waltz is the *leçon du jour* the following afternoon. The Polish couple, both tall and model-thin, demonstrate dance moves with precision but without apparent enjoyment, and never a smile. They insist their students adhere to the Eastern European instruction style – starting the dance on the right foot rather than the left, for instance – which, for the Westerner, makes what should be a fun lesson a chore. The group protests. The duo becomes angry. Fritz, who knows a bit of Polish, tells the couple he and his colleague will teach the class. They agree and leave.

Later, over soft drinks in the bar, Inga mentions how friendly Fritz has become with her husband.

"Yes, I've noticed," David replies. "Well, they both grew up in the same region, both went to the States and became successful. Fritz is very bright, as is Otto. So, a lot in common. And look at you, with your own practice. You're right up there with them. I assume you got your degree?"

"Yes, with honors. In practice five years now."

"And you enjoy it?"

"Very much. I've written two books on how I treat my patients – a simple approach that works good. If you like, I'll tell you a little about it."

"Okay, but no big words."

She glances at her watch. "I'll be short."

"Most psychological problems," she begins, "phobias, anxiety, depression, are because of an imbalance between three core areas in our body." Her appearance changes as she speaks: a furrow now traces across her forehead; a comfortable slouch straightens; her voice is brisk. A mien of seriousness has taken hold.

"Really? And they are?"

She looks about the empty lounge. Most have been enticed to the decks by the abundant sun and the saltwater pool. Tom pops his head in briefly, glances around, waves to David and leaves. A moment later he passes by the window on one of his frequent power walks around the ship.

Assured of privacy, Inga uncrosses her legs, spreading them wide enough to allow her to place David's hand between them. "This core deals with making babies, of course, but also gives the satisfaction of sex and physical intimacy. Probably the most common problem I see," – she re-crosses her legs and brings his hand into the valley of her chest – "this area relates to the heart: the emotions, kindness, love, sadness, guilt." She points to her forehead. "Finally, the brain: intelligence, reasoning, logic, all start here. These three areas must be in balance. Of course, there is overlap, but with questions I find out the principal problem area. On this I concentrate. Fix the big one, and the others fall in line. That, in a nutshell, is how I practice. What do you think?"

"Inga," David says, his tone semi-serious, "Could you run through them again?"

She laughs. "You make fun, but I have very good results. I'd love to send you one of my books, but it's in German."

"Way beyond me. But one last question."

"Is this a joke? I'm serious about what I do." Her frown reappears.

"So I see, but no, I'm just curious."

Two couples, all in bathing suits, pass by and nod. David stands as though to leave, but leans to whisper in her ear. "And you, my dear – are you in balance, everything aligned?"

She grins and beckons him to her. Her voice, on the verge of laughter, returns the whisper: "One area is lacking badly. And, if you haven't guessed, that's what I want you for."

Every cruise has its own vibration – a rhythm that establishes itself as the days pass. When the majority of passengers seem to be on the same page, singing the same song, it may be recognized by nothing more than eruptions of laughter during dinner, clusters of people late in the evening deep in conversation, a full dance floor, the repartee during trivia, or not having to explain a joke at the bar. Like pornography, it's hard to describe but you know it when it's there. Ask a crew member and he'll say the same.

When this vibe is absent there's a dissonance, like an orchestra out of tune. As someone who has been in both camps, David feels that this contingent of travelers is as one, clearly in harmony.

"Are you married, David?"

They are sitting in the theater, with an empty seat between them. Stage workers are setting things up for the evening's entertainment.

"Yes," David replies, "just short of seven years. Long enough to realize it isn't for me."

"Kids?"

David shakes his head no. *Except*, he thinks, *for the three-year-old we lost. Daddy's little girl. The memory too raw to remember, never mind talk about.*

"This is good. No need to put them through it. I know about that. And your work – what is your business?"

"Don't have one. Retired about two years ago."

"But you look young to retire. Do you have enough" – she hesitates – "enough...?"

"Money? Yes, I do." He pauses. "And since you asked, I'll tell you a quick story that very few – in fact, no one – knows. But if you tell anyone, I'll deny it. And then, of course, I'll have to kill you."

She returns his laugh. "I listen to secrets every day," she says as she reaches over and takes his hand. "I'm a good listener. I want to hear."

"How's the time – you know – Otto?"

"Fine. Even if he walks in, we're just talking."

He hesitates for a moment, then after a quick scan of the theater, settles into his seat. "Okay. It all began when I was in the military, the Air Force. I worked as an accountant. Not exciting, but that was my degree from college, and I owed the government time. I'm very good at numbers, and it wasn't long before it was noticed. Soon I was being sent to Air Force bases all over the world. I audited their books and sent the results back to headquarters. This went on for a while, got a couple of promotions, then I was sent to the Middle East. Okay so far? Not boring you?"

"No, I let you know." She is turned toward him, chin cupped in her hands, engrossed in the telling.

"The new job was to review every contract over a half-million dollars that the Air Force was negotiating with local contractors and vendors – things like housing complexes, malls, sports facilities, entire bases, real big stuff, most running into millions of dollars. Nothing moved on the project until I signed off."

"Much responsibility," she says. "You did good job?"

"Yes, evaluations were always superior. Then when it got around that my audit, in most every instance, determined who got the contract, a lot of very generous offers came my way. I put them off for a while, but eventually said, 'What the hell?' and went for the money. I insisted on a percentage – three to five percent, depending on the number of bids of the total project. The money was wired to banks in the Bahamas, Germany, England, and even your country, Inga."

"You'll have to call me when you visit." Her voice is teasing. "And they couldn't be traced?"

"I mixed the real accounts with dozens that led nowhere. It would take years to sort them out. And even if someone became suspicious, they would find nothing in the paperwork. I'm very good at what I do – better than anyone who might investigate."

"So why quit?"

"Because people were my weak link – the ones I was dealing with. They had me in their pockets. Eventually, greed kicks in. They'd be demanding more and paying less. It's all about timing. I decided to fold it up. I had all I'd ever need. So, I resigned from the military. Honorable discharge, incidentally."

"What a very good story. And you got away with it! I am jealous!" Her face is flushed.

Interesting, David thinks, noticing the sparkle in her eyes, the undivided attention, no mention of stealing or breaking laws, just excited about how it all went down. *She'd have been a great Bonnie for Clyde.*

"But you don't act like a rich man."

"And I won't for a couple more years. No flaunting. Don't want to raise suspicions just in case someone wonders how I got so wealthy all of a sudden."

"You're a smart man, David. Seems I'm surrounded by them." She puts her head back and runs both hands through her hair. A smile crosses her face. "It's funny, but in a way, I have a like situation. Since marrying Otto, I invest, not money, nothing hidden, just playing the game, being a good wife, attractive for him socially, a perfect hostess, faithful as far as he knows, always building up my account. When he dies – and already he has problems of health – I'll be very wealthy."

"Any weak links?"

"Yes. Me with people like you, my Yankee *doppelganger*, and my friend back home. But, like you, I cover my tracks well. But talking now, and looking back, I still don't understand why Otto picked me." She puts up her hand. "Before you think I look for compliments, I don't. Listen, David, with his wealth, he could get many women to do the things I do."

"So how come you?" David wonders aloud.

"I think he sees in me difficulty. I cannot think of an English word."

"Challenge?" David suggests.

"Yes, exactly. A challenge I was from the beginning. He knew I am a free spirit, not likely to do as told. This difficulty he found attractive. The harder the battle, the more he finds pleasure if he wins. Like," she adds, "the cowboys in your country who ride wild horses and got them to settle down and behave."

"And did he succeed?"

"Would I be here with you?"

"So he's got a tiger by the tail, like an old song goes. What do you think would happen if he were to catch on to you?"

"I don't know. Way down, he doesn't trust me. I even think, David, sometimes he's had me followed. But also I am sure he doesn't want to lose me, have me walk away. So maybe he even does nothing, just puts up with it." She shrugs her shoulders. "But right now I don't think about that. I just want to enjoy with you the few days we have. I am a witch," she adds, smiling, "very psychic – I sense we'd get along the first day we meet. I feel some uneasiness about us also, but I'm not going to worry about it now."

With roommate Fritz encamped, either reading or napping in the cabin, meetings – sometimes only minutes – continue in various locations on the ship: the theater when available, the library, a cul-de-sac on the third deck behind the smokestacks, a portion of the lounge that closes during the day, and, when possible, a space off the passageway at the side of the stage.

This room, shrouded by a large damask drape, is used to store unneeded stage equipment: props from past shows, all manner of decorations, cue cards and colored lights that fill two large gray boxes, costumes yellowed with age hanging on sagging racks, a broken microphone, tangles of electric cord. The entire dust-laden scene is illuminated by a single bulb dangling from the ceiling. There, shouldered between unyielding detritus, they meet. Standing is the only position available to them.

The privacy does allow Inga to display her formidable breasts – absent discernible sag and surgical intervention – and, with a practiced zip, her impressive derrière. Inga feels as well as she looks. Efforts are made to improve body alignment but unfortunately, the contortions are more embarrassing than effective. Ardor is also dampened by voices in the lounge, easily heard through the adjoining wall.

Concluding their exertions, Inga exits through the theater, David via the door leading to the lounge. On one occasion he notices an unfinished cup of tea and a flattened lemon wedge in the ashtray at a nearby table.

The sea days continue as a run of calm waters and clear, cloudless days. Approaching the equator, most passengers seek the deck. Some favor the shade of umbrellas. Others, bodies oiled and glistening, bras askew, marinate on towel-draped deck chairs, with the pool and showers available for cooling down. Attentive waiters provide towels, snacks, and drinks.

Passing through the mid-deck lounge on such a day, David sees Margaret in her usual spot chatting with one of the crew. A few tables away, Otto is reading, the book balanced on his protruding belly. *Might as well get this over with*, David thinks. *See where I stand.*

Approaching Otto's table, he sees Margaret take out her compact and begin to powder her nose. David smiles to himself. *That old gossip, I bet she's watching in the mirror.*

He reaches Otto and peers over him. "Mind if I join you, sir?" David asks nervously. "Unless you can't leave a good story."

Otto removes his glasses and looks up. "Oh, the dancer," he says. "Sit down. Please, call me Otto." A lightly garnished accent is evident, but his English is excellent.

David remarks on Otto's comfortable facility with the language. Otto mentions English as a requirement in Swiss secondary schools, but explains that he gained proficiency in America.

"Where in the States?" A few couples have entered the lounge. The afternoon tea service is beginning.

"Boston. I got my doctorate in chemistry at MIT. Had a wonderful time. Was offered a job in the States, but my heart was in Switzerland. So back I came, and into the pharmaceutical business." His eyes, blue and friendly, fit well in an open, well-formed face.

"Inga tells me you've done well in business."

"Yes, very well. Better than I could have imagined. And," he pauses, "since you brought Inga up – I would have if you hadn't – some discussion is probably due."

"A handsome lady," David replies, nodding. "A good dancer."

A server approaches with an assortment of teas, finger sandwiches, and a tower of sweets. Otto makes a tea selection, reaches for a chocolate-covered cherry, hesitates, and requests the waiter to bring a wedge of lemon. "Touch of diabetes," he says. "Must be careful."

"Where were we?" Otto continues. "Ah, yes, a good dancer. I know, but beyond that, she likes you." He raises his hand as David attempts to interrupt. "Let me finish. I have no problem with the occasional dance or two. You both look well when you do. Although, I must confess, the closeness bothers me somewhat."

"We only do what seems to fit the song. Surprised you noticed."

"David, I notice everything regarding my wife."

"You have nothing to be concerned about."

"Possibly not," he continues, as though not hearing, "but when someone tampers, innocent or not, with someone or something I love – and I do love her, David – I get angry."

"Otto, it's..."

He raises his hand again, this time more abruptly. "And my instinct is to get even. But before that, I attempt to resolve the situation, not let it fester, not let it become worse. Whatever the problem, I am very honest with the people responsible for my concern – as I'm doing with you – as I have done dozens of times in business. I must say, though, that when it involves my wife – someone, I repeat, I care deeply for – it takes on added urgency."

As David listens, he feels that the man sitting before him, his fleshy jaw in a determined set, eyes now cold, is someone whose company he would probably enjoy if the circumstances were different. David feels a frisson of pity for the poor bastard, here in the late afternoon of his life, having to confront interlopers like himself – the indignity, all for a woman waiting for him to die. A sad thing.

"And if you can't resolve it, let's say, in business, then what do you do?" David asks.

The waiter returns with a lemon wedge. Otto squeezes a few drops into his tea, stirs the half-filled cup, and takes a sip. His smile is baleful. "I do what has to be done."

"Well, in this instance, Otto, there's nothing to be concerned about."

"Perhaps. In any case, thank you for listening." He pauses. "But we do understand each other, do we not?"

"We understand each other very well."

"Good. I must be getting back to my book."

Recalling their conversation later – and the not-so-subtle threat – David is pleased to be plowing through the Atlantic Ocean, 150 miles off the coast of Africa, and not on the home turf of one possessive husband.

The next morning, Inga passes him in the buffet line, pausing long enough to offer a good morning and a whispered, "Pool bar, noon." *Unusual place to be meeting*, David thinks. *Probably the busiest area of the ship at that hour.*

The conversation is brief. "Otto is greatly upset," she says, "mean, calling me names, which is not usual. So we see no more of each other until I settle him down. When things are better, I will contact with you."

Without a further glance, she turns and heads toward the pool.

The cruise is at the mid-point of its itinerary, and most passengers have found their comfort zone. It's also at this juncture David and Fritz have identified the passenger cohort they'll be primarily dealing with – or not – the remainder of the voyage. They have encountered the single ladies whose refusal to dance is set in concrete, those formerly disinclined who are now amenable to "a spin around around the floor," and the enthusiasts who feel a song not danced to is a wasted one. Married ladies' participation in the activity is husband-contingent and can change on a nightly basis; that group is best played by ear.

A similar culling occurs with the socializing aspect of the gentlemen host position: those passengers who frequently invite the men to join them for a drink and chat; others who desire less regular interaction; and those who consistently prefer their own company and companions.

True to her word, Inga goes missing, absent at dance lessons and pre-sentations in the theater. Evenings she is deep in conversation with Otto or ensconced with others at a table in the back of the lounge, often with Fritz in attendance. No glances are exchanged. *Perhaps*, David thinks, *our little romance is over.* To his surprise, he feels bad about this. Despite her (and his) teenage behavior, the woman is undeniably intelligent and stylishly elegant – qualities he feels are as essential to seduction as lust and dry martinis.

The next landfall is at the islands of Sao Tome and Principe off the coast of Gabon, situated a kilometer north of the equator. A native bar-becue has been arranged at nearby Boom Boom Island. There a trio of small buildings rings a central, cleared area. Sheltered by banyan trees, the barbecue pit, trailing smoke, is being tended by natives. Diminutive waves lap a broad, white beach. In the distance the ocean shimmers in the heat of midday. David joins the others in the invigorating water. Waiters – young men in white shirts, red bow ties, and Madras swimming trunks – circulate among the swimmers with trays of drinks.

Inga, Otto, and their cohort have established themselves at the far end of the beach just before dense vegetation overtakes it. The thought of a stroll in her direction, perhaps for a swimsuit photo, David rejects as ill-advised. Later, during the meal, they brush by each other. A small smile is expected, but lips so eager to be kissed two days earlier remain sealed.

After their locally inspired multi-course meal, David joins Tom on the bus ride back to the tender and onto the ship. Their conversation meanders from impressions of the cruise line to the itinerary, the menu, the wine offerings, and a variety of trip-related topics. Tom discusses his job, citing examples of bad things happening to good people who let situations get out of hand.

"You wouldn't believe," he says, shaking his head, "what men will do for a piece of ass. They think they can get away with it, but they never do."

His intense gaze is a distraction, but aside from that – and his being something of a loner – David decides he's a good guy.

Inga attends the last dance class. As David's partner during the salsa sequence, she informs him that things are better with Otto. Also, she misses him. When the dance finishes, she excuses herself and departs.

Considering their frosty relationship of late, the news of her continued interest is a relief. At that moment, David decides he's going to ride this pony to the finish, no backing off. If this makes the old man angry, so be it. *In a few days we'll be half a world apart and I'll be damned if I'm going to spend my days – or more probably nights – wondering what the end of the story might have been.*

Scenarios such as this present infrequently, and when they do, David's response has invariably aped Farragut's — "Damn the torpedoes, full speed ahead" – and he suspects Inga's of the same mind. He remembers the risks taken back in his Air Force days, but also the rush of beating the system. Otto's warning him off only upped the ante, freshened the pot. Forbidden fruit is always the sweetest. And David is determined to savor the moment.

Walvis Bay, on the coast of Namibia, is the final stop before Cape Town. The port's strategic location has provided provisions and a safe haven for voyagers rounding the Cape of Good Hope for centuries.

Dinner that evening will be served away from the ship. A convoy of all-terrain vehicles transports the full complement of passengers approximately thirty kilometers into the desert. There, encircled by a range of towering dunes, two large tents have been set up. On arrival, the passengers are greeted with drinks, hors d'oeuvres, and music supplied by a native band. Camels, with attendants, are available for rides.

While waiting for his first experience riding on a camel, David surveys the surroundings. The setting, worthy of Hollywood, is spectacular. Fortresses of sand – the tallest in the world rust-red in color inflamed by a lingering sun – stretch in all directions. One expects at any moment to see a chestnut stallion canter through the iridescence with a rider in headdress and billowing white cape who bears a startling resemblance to Peter O'Toole in *Lawrence of Arabia*.

The bar has been set up with service and drink choices, unchanged from the ship. The menu for the evening includes butterfish fillets, ostrich medallions, prawns, and vegetable curry. The Bavarian bunch, as some have named the German-Swiss-Austrian alliance, is seated apart from the rest, Fritz next to Otto and across from Inga. Since this association has developed, the friendliness Fritz and David enjoyed at the start of the voyage has been replaced with, if not hostility, then coolness. Other than short periods of conversation, they are as two strangers.

During the later stages of the meal, David notices Inga, camera in hand, walking from the tent into the desert. A circle of red lights has been placed in the sand a few hundred meters from the dining area, designating the boundaries beyond which guests are asked not to trespass. Disorientation, they are told, is a common occurrence in the desert; the lights are always to be kept in view.

Otto seems absorbed in conversation. After waiting a few minutes, David heads out. He finds Inga a short distance beyond the lights. She turns at his approach.

"I was hoping you would see me," she says. She reaches out for him. Bathed in the twilight, specks in the vastness about them, they hold each other. In David's romantic memory those few moments that night deep in the Namibian desert stand apart from the rest.

They stroll and chat. She seems tense. She agrees she is. "Before someone comes looking, I must go," she finally says. "I don't want to spoil all my work from the last few days."

"I was beginning to wonder."

"Don't worry, we are good. Also, David, be sure to dance with me the last night. I'm working on something for Cape Town." A quick kiss, and she leaves. David returns to the tents from another direction.

The captain's farewell reception is held on the last night of the cruise. He briefly introduces the senior members of the crew, but the night, appropriately, is given over to the service crew, cabin staff, waiters, bartenders, and laundry and engine-room crew, some of whom seldom see the light of day. The applause is sincere and sustained, as most crew members are seen on a daily basis, and friendships have formed.

The reception ends with a photo show. During the cruise, candid shots were taken of passengers in various situations: asleep on a deck chair, dining, dancing, on excursions off the boat, in conversation, and in a myriad of other activities. As Andrea Bocelli and Sarah Brightman join their voices in "Time to Say Goodbye," the photos are displayed on a large screen. Cheers and whoops erupt as passengers and crew are recognized. Landfalls are revisited, and shipboard activities are recalled with a thoughtful bit of nostalgia as the voyage winds down. Space has been created in the center of the dining room to allow dancing, a final opportunity for ladies to flaunt their finery, and men their tuxedoed, tanned, debonair images.

Fritz and David dine with two of the ladies they met on the first night. Their consensus: a wonderful trip, with plans made for a return within the year. A mischievous fate has placed their table next to Otto, Inga, and their group. Rather than having a wayward glance be misconstrued, David sits with his back to them.

The evening passes quickly. David and Fritz circulate about the room, busy with goodbyes and farewell dances. Behind the veneer of friendliness, David's mind is occupied with a single thought: getting Inga on the dance floor. That Otto won't allow it is a distinct possibility.

Emboldened by a significant quantity of wine, David approaches her table. He makes his request. Without a glance in his direction, Otto, with a quick flick of his hand, bids her go.

They dance to the opposite side of the floor. "Thought you would never get to ask," she begins. "He is upset. I must speak quickly. First of all, what time is your flight tomorrow?"

"At the airport by six o'clock in the evening. And you?"

"We are staying on the boat through tomorrow. He's decided to meet an owner of a company he has interest in. Gone for the day. It's like a gift."

The song ends. She crosses the floor and gestures to Otto. He smiles and waves back. In a moment the band starts another number. David and Inga continue to dance. "Okay," she says, "we are good for now. David, listen carefully. There is a hotel, the Colonial, I stayed there years ago with my first husband. It's off the tourist path and should serve us good." Her whispers are urgent. "I will meet you there at two o'clock. My name is Lucy Charette. You are an old friend coming to see me. You will need a cab."

"Are you sure about all this, Inga?"

The band is putting the final flourish to the song. Couples are leaving, gowns rustling as they pass.

Inga steps back and looks directly at David. "Yes, as sure as I've ever been. Remember, David: the Colonial Hotel, two o'clock, Lucy Charette. If you're not there by three o'clock, I'll leave." She smiles and squeezes his hand. "Sort of exciting, isn't it? Please don't make me leave."

Departing the dance floor, she stops and turns to him. "David, that man at the bar has been staring at me. Who is he?"

David glances over. "Oh, that's Tom. I think he likes you. He's mentioned you a couple of times. Consider it a compliment."

"He has never spoken to me."

David shakes his head. "Maybe just shy."

At the table David thanks Inga for the dance and wishes everyone a safe and pleasant journey home. He receives no response.

When the lounge closes at midnight, David, as is his custom on the final night of a voyage, heads to the deck with a glass of wine in hand. In a lounge chair, feet on the middle rung of the rail, he sits, sips and, as the inky water races by, reviews the trip. He endorses totally the comments of the ladies earlier:

"Marvelous weather."
"Superb dining and service."
"Convivial guests."
"Well-chosen ports of call."

The highlights, he feels, were Boom Boom Island and the Namibian desert evening – and, particularly for him, the Inga experience. Over the last few days, she has totally eclipsed his thoughts. *Can't remember,* he thinks, *when I wanted to get at a woman more than her. And there's still tomorrow.* He stands, raises his glass, makes a wish for a safe flight home, and flings it into the night.

As he passes through the lobby toward his cabin, he notices a man and woman walking down an adjoining corridor. The man is wide and tall with a glistening bald head. The woman, her arm linked with his, wears a long skirt and a rain jacket with the hood up. *I'll be damned,* David thinks. *That's Tom. Good for him. Wonder who the female is?* As they walk, the lady's dress lifts enough to expose slivers of bright red sneaker. "Naw," David says to himself, "couldn't be."

A cloudless, crisp, sunny morning welcomes the ship to Cape Town harbor. Remnants of mist cling to Table Mountain, looming large over the city. Robben Island, Nelson Mandela's prison home for years, is a smudge of brown in the distance. A trio of tugboats gently nudges the vessel between two other cruise ships to its docking space.

With his baggage safely en route to the airport, David gazes at the bustle of activity on the dock below, his arms resting on the same rail where two weeks earlier he watched the Canary Islands recede in the mist. And then the tap on his shoulder…

He notices familiar faces. Mario, the lounge pianist, and another man, unfamiliar to David, are embracing at the periphery of the crowd. A church group, seldom seen during the voyage, troops into what appears to be a school bus. Tom, standing at the far end of the dock, is in conversation with two black dockworkers. In the shade of the reception building, a native band, fronted by half a dozen brightly costumed dancers, offers a musical welcome. He recognizes Margaret, absent her cane, walking to a hotel shuttle bus. Fritz, who offered a perfunctory handshake as he departed the cabin, is nearby, pushing through the throng. David has decided he will let the rush subside; trip recollections and imagined activities for the afternoon will pass the time. Sometime later, he departs the vessel.

Just inside the entrance of the Colonial Hotel, a series of potted plants channel guests to the atrium. To the left is a wall of travel brochures and a desk with a telephone. On the opposite side, a gray vinyl couch and a coffee table strewn with magazines front a brick fireplace. A frayed red carpet leads to the reception desk. A bald stub of a man wearing a green eyeshade leans over it.

David stands before the bent figure. The man doesn't look up. "Excuse me," David says. "I'm here to see Lucy Charette. I'm expected."

"Yes," the man replies, his voice hoarse. A cigarette smolders in an ashtray at his side. He turns slightly, still half-bent, and removes a key from one of a series of hooks lining the wall. He pushes it across the wooden counter to David. "Been expecting you. The lady told me to watch out for you."

"Don't need a key.".

A shaky, thin-veined hand extends over the counter and retrieves it. His desk task apparently completed, the man straightens himself. A thin, blotched face with gray stubble comes into view. "Two-twenty-six. Elevator around the corner, far end of the corridor to your right." His lips thin to a smile.

As David waits for the elevator, the bald man back at the reception desk pushes back his visor, adjusts his glasses, and reaches for a yellow Post-it, on which is written a series of numbers. These he punches into a mobile phone. After a brief conversation, he discards the note and returns the phone to the charger cradle.

At that moment, the doors of a black car parked on the street outside the Colonial Hotel swing open.

The elevator is from an earlier day: entrance is gained by pulling aside a collapsible steel frame, which doesn't fully open, and closes with difficulty. A panel contains five buttons, the numerals of which are worn beyond identification. Assuming the place has a basement, David presses the third from the bottom.

With an abrupt jerk the elevator slowly ascends, and in a few moments comes to a grinding, jerky halt. David's guess is correct: he's on the second floor.

The door to Room 226 opens after a single knock. Her smile is one of relief. "So glad to see you," she says. "I am starting to worry." Her usual tight slacks have been replaced: a pale green sundress billows around her figure nicely. She loops her arms around his neck, her body tight to his. "Finally," she sighs. "But give me a minute. The loo first."

David sits on the edge of the bed, its covers turned back, and looks around. "Ain't the Ritz," he says to himself. The room seems designed by the same decorator who did the lobby: coffee table and magazines, vinyl couch, fold-up chairs, and TV. The floors are wooden and uncovered. The single window is open; a breeze ruffles its curtains. He hears the elevator starting its arduous climb.

Inga steps in and turns her back to him. "The zipper is stuck," she says, "and while you're there, unhook the bra." She bends over the bed. "Maybe this makes it easier."

As he moves into her softness there is a knock on the door.

"Oh, shit, David." Her hips are restless. "Don't move," she whispers. "They'll go away in a minute." The knocks continue. "Guess you'll have to." She straightens up.

David pads to the door. "Yeah, what do you want?" he asks.

"Room service. Checking if everything is fine." The voice has a strong local accent.

"Everything's good," David replies.

"Hotel rules. Checklist has to be signed. Only takes a minute."

He looks at Inga. "What do you think?"

She shrugs her shoulders. "Might as well get over with it," she whispers. "Sounds like they are not going away."

David opens the door. Looming large in front of him are two black men. Between them stands a tall white man with a bald glistening head. All are wearing black gloves.

"What in the hell are you doing here?"

"Hi, David," Tom responds. "I'm here to take the missus back to the ship. These fellows here will be visiting with you for a while." He pauses. "I tried to tell you, buddy."

David feels like he's going to be sick. A trickle of sweat runs down the center of his back. This can't be happening, he thinks. He glances at Inga. Her eyes are wide and frightened; her face is the white of alabaster.

"Put your shoes on, dearie," Tom orders her. "Your husband is waiting."

"He's not on the ship." Tears are forming in her eyes. "He's at a meeting somewhere."

"'Taint so, lady. It was a setup from the start. He wanted to see what you'd do with a free afternoon."

"Look," David interrupts, "nothing's happened. I have a few dollars. Let's make this whole thing go away. You couldn't find us and called it off. No one's to know. I can make it worth your while."

"Little late for that. The old man is aware of the whole deal."

"How could he?" Inga pipes up. "It's impossible." Her voice is anxious but, in spite of the situation, displays a hint of defiance.

"Because you told me last night," Tom continues. "When you were making your plans with Loverboy here. And I told Otto. Hey, that's what I get paid to do. He sort of knew something was brewing, but didn't know where or when."

"But I never spoke to you last night."

David interrupts, "He reads lips, Inga. Remember the stares?"

"Oh my God!" She begins to cry, her last vestige of resistance gone. "What's going to happen?" At that precise moment David is wondering the same thing. The squat, big-bellied black men take positions next to him, their arms bent with muscle.

"Tom, wait a minute." David's voice is pleading. "Five thousand dollars, any bank you want. You'll have it by morning. Just give me some time to get out of here."

"You know, David, what would happen to me if I double-crossed him?" asks Tom. "I'll tell you. Exactly what's going to happen to you in a few minutes."

"Please, Tom, I…" His voice fades.

"You're wasting your time." Tom turns to Inga. "Say goodbye to your boyfriend. Don't think you'll be seeing him again." He pauses. "Just like the one in Zürich." He laughs and shakes his head. "You know honey, you're keeping us in business."

"How do you know about him?" she asks, her voice just above a whisper.

"I'll refresh your memory just in case David here thinks he's the only fish in your pond. Maybe you remember a taxi ride you took the last time you two got together in Zürich?"

"Vaguely."

"And a lady at the train station, late for an appointment, asked to share your taxi." Inga nods. "In appreciation of your kindness, she insisted that she pick up your fare. Eventually you agreed. The taxi dropped you at your hotel, and the lady, my partner, continued on. The rest was easy."

"What's happened to him?" Concern is evident in her voice, which, even in this circumstance, bothers David.

"Beats me. Wasn't really involved in the case. Could find out, but don't really care."

Tom takes her by the arm, and they start to the door. As she passes David, she looks at him, her eyes full with tears. "I am so sorry," she mumbles, her voice hoarse.

David touches her shoulder and nods. "Me too." As she leaves, he notices that the back of her dress is still half open. *So close, so goddamn close*, he thinks. *It's going to haunt me.*

Tom nods to the men now standing on each side of David. "Okay, guys, I'm heading back to the ship. My partner will be by shortly. She'll have the rest of your money. Remember, leave the same way you came, gloves on until you're out of the building." He departs with Inga.

One of the black men decides to use the bathroom. David eyes the door, about four steps away. *Now's my chance*, he thinks. *If I can get out of this room, I bet I can outrun these walruses.* Bending as though to tie his shoes, he lunges forward. Just as he grasps the doorknob, a gloved hand tears it away.

One of the men stands behind David and pins his arms together. The other comes to the front. Then it begins. The first blow explodes his nose, the blood warm on his face. With either the second or third punch he feels his jaw crack. Soon his vision is gone. Every scream is answered with a blow to the head. He stops screaming. The men change positions. New fists collapse his chest; bones are snapping; breaths are painful gasps. All of a sudden, his body becomes numb. The blows continue, but with no feeling. The grip in back loosens. Stretched on the floor, he fights for air. Waves of gray, black, and brown wash over him like surf on a beach.

During a clearer moment, David becomes aware of a woman's voice and heels clicking on the wooden floor. Then, as blackness envelopes him: the strike of a match, the snap of a lock, the slam of a door, and the unmistakable smell of a Gauloise cigarette.

14

JONESY

DURING THE SUMMER OF 1950, while caddying at the Point Judith Country Club in Narragansett, Rhode Island, I became friendly with a kid from Wakefield, known to all as Jonesy. (I've altered the name for this story.) Although we were both fifteen, he was a few inches shorter, with a build that could only be described as scrawny. "About a hundred pounds," was his estimation. Occasionally, he went to the racetrack in Pawtucket and worked as an exercise boy walking horses. His ambition was to become a jockey.

Jonesy was a sad-looking kid, pimply and pale, with shaggy, home-cut hair, usually off by himself reading a comic book. Seldom with a lunch or soft drink, he wore the same T-shirt, trousers, and unlaced brown sneakers for weeks. His front teeth were blackened with cavities. Hollowed cheeks gave his face the pinched look of an older person. He looked like a kid who hadn't caught many breaks in life. I felt sorry for Jonesy.

From kids talking, I learned his mother had a reputation and a nickname: "Two-Bit Annie."

One evening, after caddying together that afternoon, we walked to the main road, where he hitched a ride to Wakefield. He mentioned along the way that he hoped his mother would be home to make supper.

"Jonesy," I said, "I live just down the road. Come eat with us. Someone will take you home afterward."

He declined the invitation as being "too much trouble," but after some coaxing, he was soon seated at our kitchen table, putting away a meal that would make a longshoreman proud.

My grandmother served strawberry shortcake for dessert – hollowed-out biscuits filled with slices of blood-red strawberries, drowned in mounds of freshly whipped cream. "Hope you enjoy it," she said.

He never looked up. As though vacuumed, the treat disappeared in seconds. Sporting a dab of cream on the tip of his nose, he picked up the bowl and slurped down the remaining juice.

"Well, Jonesy," my grandmother said, "what do you think?"

The grin on his face said it all. Jonesy seldom smiled, too embarrassed to show his teeth. "We have this at home all the time," he said. "Just like this."

My grandmother and aunt shared a smile. They both knew that may not have been true – I had spoken of Jonesy in the past. I wondered if he had even seen strawberry shortcake before.

When he left, he thanked my grandmother. "That was the best dessert I ever had."

"Glad you enjoyed it," she said. "Come again."

And he did.

When my aunt learned of his jockey aspirations, she gave him a book about Eddie Arcaro, a great rider during the 1950s. On his next visit, she quizzed him about the story. It became apparent that Jonesy hadn't read the book – because he couldn't. At age fifteen, he was in fifth grade. The only printed material he understood was in the form of comics; the pictures gave him a clue as to the meaning of the words.

When we took Jonesy home, he always asked to be let off at the corner of Main Street and Kenyon Avenue in Wakefield. "I live just up there," he said, pointing to a row of well-tended, attractive homes. We hadn't imagined Jonesy living in such an upscale neighborhood.

On one such drop-off, my aunt stopped at one of the local stores for a purchase. Later, driving along Main Street, we saw Jonesy just ahead, about to turn down River Street, at that time one of the less desirable sections of town. Jonesy, it seemed, was ashamed of a lot of things in his life.

Kids can be cruel. In our caddy environment, where large chunks of time were spent waiting, there was plenty of opportunity to hone that skill. The insults and taunts – either received or given – were not restricted to either blacks or whites. But in any group, there is usually one who is more aggressive, more brutal, than the rest. In ours, Norm was that kid.

He was black, a halfback on the high school football team and bigger than the rest of us – T-shirt taut over a wide chest, neck a wedge of muscle – the proverbial fire hydrant. Jonesy, one of Norm's favorite targets, never reacted to the crap Norm laid on him; he just concentrated on his comic book or walked away.

One midsummer day, the course was quiet – the caddies just hanging out, restless with inactivity. Jonesy and I were playing cards.

With little else to do, Norm came over and began his rant. "How's old Two-Bit these days, Jonesy?" he began. "Still doing everyone in town?"

Jonesy put down his cards, stood up and walked away.

Norm followed him. "Grease her up and she's good for a half dozen," Norm said, laughing. "Ain't that right, Jonesy?"

Jonesy was edging toward the road.

Norm trailed a couple of feet behind. "Yeah, your ma's got one busy body. That's what I hear." Norm was loving it. He had an audience. Everyone was watching the show.

Norm kept at him, the insults more personal, more gross. Everyone thought Jonesy would have bolted up the road by now, or Norm, having gotten his fill, would call it off. But the abuse continued.

Suddenly Jonesy stopped and turned around; a woeful wisp of a kid, his skinny body trembling, he stood stock-still and faced his tormentor. Norm closed in. Jonesy disappeared behind the massive shoulders and upper body of the halfback.

All of a sudden, a thin arm and a clenched hand, heading in the direction of Norm's face, came into view. Norm, not expecting it, didn't duck or change position. It landed squarely on his nose.

Norm looked stunned. Jonesy hadn't moved, as though waiting for whatever was in store. Norm reached to grab him. At that precise moment, blood began to flow from his nose, a dribble to start but soon a torrent. He took off his T-shirt, balled it up, and pressed it against his face, then stumbled to a bench by the table and lay down.

With Norm tending to his nose, I grabbed Jonesy, and we headed up the road. No one followed. We slowed the pace.

"What in the hell did you do that for? He's going to kill you."

"I don't care. If I get beat up, I get beat up." He looked at me straight on. "I just couldn't take it no more."

As we walked, Jonesy talked about his mother – first time ever. "I know what she does when she sends me to the movies," he said. "I ain't stupid. But she can't get a job. No one will hire her."

We had almost reached the highway when Jonesy stopped. "You know," he said, "I try to help her, so she don't have to do that stuff. I gave her my caddy money, but she wouldn't take it. She cried the first time."

"How come?"

"I don't know. But I don't want her to feel bad. Now I just buy stuff I know she needs and leave it on the table."

We continued to the main road. In all the time I had known Jonesy, I had never heard him talk so much. Nor did he seem upset with what happened back at the club or the beating he was sure to get when Norm caught up with him. He seemed almost proud of what he had done – maybe for one of the few times in his life.

Jonesy went back to the course the next day, knowing what was probably in store for him – a pretty gutsy move.

But a funny thing happened: nothing. For a start, Norm wasn't there. Jonesy caddied two rounds and went home. A week or so later, Norm turned up but said little. The only change – no one picked on Jonesy again.

When I turned sixteen I took a better paying job in Galilee.. About the same time, Jonesy became more involved in horse racing. I heard he achieved his ambition and became a jockey. I've often wondered how things turned out for my friend – especially when I'm enjoying a dessert strewn with strawberries and mounds of freshly whipped cream.

15

A Meeting at Sandymount Strand

THE TIDE AT ITS EBB widened the beach while a ruffle of white surf lined the dark water. As banks of gray clouds raced across the darkening sky, a brisk wind funneled brown sand onto the promenade, spiraling down the walkway to a line of benches where Stephen was seated. On this late autumn afternoon, the pavilion was deserted. A rusted gate blocked its entrance, the length of beach solitary.

"Meet me at Sandymount Strand," she said. "I'll go there after work." Her voice was pleasant; perhaps he only imagined an urgency. But an uneasiness persisted.

They met that spring at a popular – at least in the 1960's – Dublin dance hall, the Crystal Ballroom – its pride a large dimpled globe that revolved over the center of the floor. Slivers of light scattered over the dancers and the gray paneled walls, which on warm nights reeked of sweat and cigarettes. A quartet – two guitars, piano and drums – provided the music.

That night Stephen noticed her standing at the edge of the dance floor talking with another woman, much older than she. Though a distance away she was immediately attractive: taller than the ladies about her she stood erect without stoop or bend, black unadorned hair falling to her shoulders. A black skirt and colored blouse completed the image. When the chat was interrupted by a man – balding, with a substantial belly – who invited her companion onto the dance floor a quick scurry around the perimeter of the hall brought Stephen within striking distance. She agreed to dance.

All of Stephen's seventy-three-inch height was needed to put him at eye level with his partner, the advantage of that: it placed him at the same latitude as the rest of her. With her comfortably nestled in the hollow of his shoulder, their bodies melded nicely. *This one,* he thought, *might be fun to get to know a little better.*

"Come here every Thursday," she said in reply to Stephen's question. "Only a half crown Tuesdays and Thursdays. Smashing place, don't ya think?" Her speech was of Dublin city: harsh, quick bursts of sound without inflection. While we danced Jo quietly sang along with the music. At those times the rough, abrasive tones of her voice softened, the grating twang replaced with a sweet-sounding lilt, more in keeping with her demure appearance. It reminded Stephen of a stutterer who's fractured speech becomes clear when words are replaced with lyrics.

Stephen nodded. First names were exchanged. Jo, he learned, was short for Josephine. "Got a cousin named Stephen," she told him, "even looks a bit like ya, tall, blonde and skinny. But you wear it better like they say."

Dancing was her favorite thing to do, the Crystal her favorite hall. "Like the crowd that comes to the place," she said. "Always a good band. Lot of good dancers. Met me first boyfriend Cormac here." She paused, a jot of distraction in her eyes. "A real chancer he was. We broke up a while back, case ya wondrin'." As though to be rid of the thought she turned to Stephen and smiled. Neither the flickering lights, powdered cheeks or lines of mascara could disguise a face flawless as porcelain, delicate in its symmetry. Wide, deep eyes hinted of innocence. Stephen wondered if she realized her beauty.

Their meetings at the Crystal provided bits of history. Jo was eighteen and worked in the stockroom at Clery's Department Store on O'Connell Street. Five days a week she walked there from her home in Ringsend, a working-class neighborhood bordering the port of Dublin, about twenty minutes away. Her father worked the docks. She told Stephen she wanted to move to England and get a job and maybe meet someone nice and get married. He wondered if she'd need a dispensation from the church to marry an Englishman. "No," she told him, laughing. "All the Irish men, the young ones anyways, are movin over there to work. Ain't nothin' around here. Making good money they are. It's them I want to meet." Stephen told her he was working at the Rotunda hospital and was from the States. "No shit," she replied, an apparent reference to his accent.

They dated sporadically through the summer; the infrequency – though discouraging serious notions – managed to foster an impatient lust, not satisfied until their last meeting here at the strand.

The wind blowing cool off the Irish Sea sharpened the air. Standing to button his coat Stephen saw her, a patch of brown far down the beach. Past pools of water reflecting a leaden sky he hurried toward her.

"Almost didn't see you, Jo." She turned, black hair streamed over her face; dark eyes met his for an instant then flicked away. A brown coat was draped over her shoulders, its cloth belt hanging at her waist. He kissed her cheek, moist with mist, studded with bits of brown sand. "Been a while, Jo." He hesitated. "Anyway you're looking great, like always."

"Look," she said, pointing towards the bay, "been watching the little boat. Trying to make port before the storm."

"Better hurry up," replied Stephen, nodding toward the dark clouds gathering over Howth Head. "Probably will make it. Almost at the power station."

Stephen took a deep breath. "Anyway Jo, you surprised me with the call. Everything all right?"

"Something I need to tell ya," she said. "We'll walk awhile, talk later."

They followed the swath of firm sand just above the tide line, the hum of the sea sharpened by the slap of waves and small stones tumbling in their wash. The few words spoken spun away, lost in the wind. Stephen tried to hold her hand. She would have none of it. *Not a good sign. What's up,* he wondered.

The broad sweep of strand began to narrow beginning its turn to the sea and the rocky promontory at its far end. Stephen thought of their last time here, the late afternoon of a brilliant summer day: families picnicking, couples strolling, children playing in the shallows; young men in bathing suits, bodies white, excepting their arms, rough housing in the surf.

Into the long twilight they played like the children around them, wading and splashing in the water; her loose skirt hiked high, white legs flushed pink in the waning sun, blouse matted with spray.

Later, in a rock bordered cul-de-sac they sat and watched the remains of the day inch into an indigo sea. The crowds had thinned, the remaining few far down the beach. "Nice afternoon," he said. She agreed. Stephen pushed aside the tangle of hair from her face and laid her head on a quickly gathered pillow of sand. Her lips – soft, yielding – tasted of salt. He fumbled with the buttons of her blouse. "Need some help?" she asked. Soon only darkness covered them.

A scattering of dunes marked the end of the beach They stopped. Jo turned toward the sea. "Guess our little boat made it." Stephen didn't answer but reached for her shoulders and turned her so they were face to face.

"Okay, Jo. We've had our walk. What's going on?"

"Maybe," she answered, "I just wanted to see ya. A friendly visit. It's been almost three months you know." Her tone was flippant, the sarcasm evident.

"Really busy at school, Jo, had a couple of exams. Hospital stuff."

She turned on him, eyes flashing. "Bullshit me boyo. Found the time didn't ya when it was me arse you wanted. Plenty popular I was before the knickers came down." Her laugh was more a sneer. "Ain't it always the way with ye chancers. Get ya little bit and ya gone." Her words spit out as though bitter on her tongue.

"Yeh, you're right, Jo. It's just I can't get off like I used to. But I'll make it up. You'll see." He reached for her. She pushed his hand away.

"Anyway," she replied, "water under the bridge."

"So what is it you want to tell me?" he asked, his tone insistent.

She reached over and straightened the lapel on his coat. "Well," she said, "I missed me friend the last two months." Stephen felt his stomach tighten. "Went for tests." She paused. "Guess what?"

Stephen shook his head.

"I'm pregnant."

My God, he thought, *it can't be.* He covered his face with his hands, fingers cold on his scalp. "You sure?"

Jo nodded, "And there ain't been no one else. I'll take any tests you like."

"But you said it was all right, back then."

"Didn't count right I guess."

Stephen felt his legs shaking. "Not shitten' me. You're being straight right?"

"I'm telling you straight. Wish I wasn't."

"Jesus, Jo, I've got to sit down."

She spread the brown coat on the sand. "What are you" – He hesitated – "what are we going to do?"

"We," she said, "are going to have a kid, that's what." She turned away, curling her knees into her chest. Black hair spilled over her face, shoulders trembling.

"Look Jo, the hospital I work in. Maybe I could find someone. There's a nurse..."

Her head jerked up sharply. "I fecked up but there'll be no murdrin."

Stephen's mouth was dry, his voice a rasp. "Okay. Look, I don't want you to do something you don't want to." He paused, "I'll work something out. Do what I have to do."

She appeared to have heard the words but her forehead had drawn into a crease, eyes fixed in a stare, like someone trying to retrieve something from memory, as an actor might his lines. And apparently she succeeded for suddenly her gaze was full on him.

"Do?" she sneered. "What the feck can ya do, a student poorer than me and me six pounds a week. Anyway, where'll ya be in a few months. The one that's going to do so much for me?"

So far away from here, honey, you'll never find me. "Back in the States, I guess," he replied.

"Righto, and me stuck here." She covered her face with her hands, muffling sobs, palms grinding into her eyes. In a choked voice she told him of the shame it would bring on her family, people talking behind her back, boys calling her a slut. "D'ya not have any feelings at all," she cried out, her voice breaking, "leaven' me this way?"

Stephen stood up, pulled her to her feet and looked directly into her eyes, which, though red and swollen, seemed dry. "1 said I'd do what I need to do."

"Ya would?" The look of surprise on her face seemed genuine. "You'd stick with me?"

He shrugged his shoulders.

Over the bay black clouds were filling voids of gray, the occasional shaft of light thrusting between them, the wind flattening swaths of choppy sea. Jo wiped her nose with the edge of her coat..

"Anyway ya don't have to do nothing."

"What do you mean?"

"I'll take care of things."

He looked at her closely. "What are you talking about, take care of things?"

"Work as long as I can; winter's coming. This old coat," she said smiling, "can hide a lot." She took his hand. "You see, I got a friend in Liverpool. She'll take me in, won't let on. I'll have the kid and let it go for adoption. I might even stay there. Find a job." She paused. "So what d'ya think?"

Stephen shut his eyes. *Oh good, sweet Jesus,* he thought, *thank you.* He wanted to fall on the sand, pound it with his fists.

"Sounds like a good idea," he answered evenly.

"But," she hesitated, "I'm going to need help. I ain't got nothing saved, and out of work all those months." She looked at him, eyes imploring. Her hand tightened on his.

"How much do you think you'll need?"

"'Bout a hundred and fifty pounds."

"Jesus, Jo, that's a lot of money. "

She dropped his hand. "Then how in the feck can I do it? Maybe," she said, "I should keep the little bastard. Let you support it for a few years. See how much that'll cost ya. This is a feckin' bargain I'm offerin'."

160

Stephen turned away. The squalls sweeping in from the sea felt good on his face. The bay was empty. *A hundred and fifty pounds,* he thought, *four hundred and fifty dollars. No way can I get that kind of money. But promise it anyway, promise her anything. Need some time to think. Got to find a way out of this.*

He looked back at her. "OK, Jo, you're right," he said. "I'll get it somehow. Will take a month or so."

"And ya won't let me down? I got your word?"

"I said I wouldn't."

"Then you got a month. Agreed?"

"Agreed."

"So that's done." Relief was in her voice. She looked at her watch. "I've got to go; they'll be wondrin' at home."

Stephen shook the sand from her coat and draped it over her shoulders.

"One more thing," she added. "I don't want to be paradin' down to your hospital with me belly pushed out, looking for me boyfriend and the money he owes me. So seal it up in a manila envelope, leave it at me work. That way I won't have to look at ya sad face, the boyo that never gave a damn about me. Ain't I right?"

Yes, my dear. Stephen thought, *you are dead right. It really was all about your arse, like you said.* "Whatever you want," he answered quietly. "But I won't forget you. We were good together."

She hesitated as if to say something, then shook her head like she had changed her mind.

"I'm leaving so. Stay here until I'm gone."

She leaned forward, brushed his cheek with her lips then turned and walked away, the coat belt dragging in the sand. Suddenly she stopped, and shouted back, "And ya woulda stuck with me?"

Stephen nodded. She smiled and continued down the beach.

He watched until she finally passed beneath the orange glow of the light at the far end of the promenade. Then, he screamed: at the sky, at the sea – until he could scream no more.

The phone kiosk at Cranfield Place was empty. Jo waited for the call to go through.

"Cormac?"

"How did it go?"

"All set. Worked just like ya said it would."

"How much?

She paused. "A hundred. It'll take about a month. Maybe we can put some away, for us."

"I want to see it first," he replied. "Did he ask questions? Like you getting shagged by somebody else? Wanted proof?"

"No, he believed me. Scared shitless he was. Ya shoulda seen me, Cormac, a regular Siobhan McKenna* And Cormac, listen to this. He said he woulda seen it through. Wouldna dumped me."

"What a feckin' ejiit." He laughed again. "Anyway, good job."

"You gonna call me tonight, Cormac?"

There was no answer; the line was dead.

Jo pulled her coat around her and tied the wet, sandy belt around her waist. Her face, a smudge of white, reflected in the fogged glass. She pushed open the kiosk door and stepped into the night.

*A versatile Irish actress known for her portrayal of Shaw's *Saint Joan*.

16

DRINKS AT DAVY'S

ONE WOULDN'T EXPECT A BAR to be this crowded at noon, even in Dublin. That, Brian suspected, must be the precise thought the woman, wedged against the door through which she had just passed, must be having at the moment. As she took in the scene, perhaps wondering if she should leave or stay, her pretty brow had the wrinkle of uncertainty. But her hesitation was short-lived; a decision had apparently been made. She removed her sunglasses, tucking them into the pouch slung over her shoulder and with a fixed, pleasant expression in place, began her assault on the knot of drinkers directly in her path. Tentative shoulder taps and gentle prods neither moved the mass or prompted a glance in her direction. A similar impasse was found no matter the direction of her efforts.

Brian, deep into the crush along the bar, watched her futility. A Yank for sure, he figured: clean-cut, blonde, a cheerleader type whose smile would undoubtedly feature straight white teeth. An image of her shaking pompoms and doing splits at a Saturday afternoon football game somewhere in the Midwest came to mind.

Several unsuccessful attempts later, the woman's frustration became obvious. The pleasant smile was no longer, her forehead was gathered in a frown. She turned to leave. About to pull open the heavy, wooden door, she glanced back for a final look. Brian, taller than most around him, raised his glass in her direction, and with his free hand pointed to a space near him. The woman hesitated, then smiled and nodded. Pushing through the scrum, Brian reached for her outstretched hand and navigated her to his spot at the bar.

"Can't be timid with this crowd," he said. "You could die of thirst."

The woman smiled and gazed around. "What's happening?"

"Rugby international at Lansdowne Road," he said. "The Welsh are over. Those wearing something red would be them. Crazy bunch. Here for a bit of pre-match lubrication. They'll be heading off soon."

Not a bad-looking woman, he thought. Tall enough to reach his shoulder, wide-set blue eyes, full, pink-glossed lips, she quite nicely filled the floppy, white Oxford shirt knotted at her waist. A wedge of tanned skin was displayed a shade lighter than her khakis.

"For the rescued a drink," Brian said. "What'll it be?"

"I don't know," she replied. "A bit early, don't you think?"

"Rule of the bar," he answered, laughing. "If you don't have a glass in at least one hand, you'll be asked to leave."

"In that case, maybe something light."

"A Gordon's and Schweppes would be the thing, then. Hardly a drink at all." Brian caught the barman's eye, pointed to his empty stout glass, and shouted above the din that the lady would have a gin and tonic.

"Now that the essentials are taken care of" – he extended his hand – "I'm Brian."

"And I'm Trish." Her smile was easy, teeth as suspected. He noticed a wedding band by the side of a large diamond.

"So, Trish, what brings you to dirty ol' Dublin and this godforsaken excuse for a pub?"

"A couple of reasons."

By the time the drinks arrived, Brian had learned that she came from upstate New York (disproving his Midwest prediction) and had graduated from Bates College in 1957 ("Yes, I was a cheerleader. How did you know?") with a major in English literature. She had written a paper on Joyce's *Ulysses* and wanted to visit Davy Byrnes, where Mr. Bloom took his lunch that memorable day.

"And here you are," said Brian, "bellying up to the same bar." He raised his glass. "To Molly and Leopold."

Trish's smile widened to a laugh. Her blue eyes crinkled. "Hear, hear," she said, raising her glass. Their glasses touched. As she brought the drink to her lips, her glance held his for an instant.

"And what's the other?" he asked.

"The other?" Her brow furrowed.

"The other reason you're here."

"Oh." She paused. "I'm on my honeymoon."

"I beg your pardon?"

"You heard right," she replied, laughing. "Ten days into it."

"And where, might I ask, is the other principal?"

"Playing golf at . . . um . . . Ballybunion. Does that sound right?"

Brian nodded a "yes." So . . ." His tone turned mock serious. "We have a new bride drinking gin and tonic with a stranger in the middle of the day in very questionable surroundings, and your husband . . ." He paused.

"Peter," she said.

"And Peter's out thrashing around the glens and grouse of Ballybunion."

Trish nodded. "And you can add that the bride is enjoying herself."

"With all due respect, my Yankee lass," Brian said, a smile belying the sternness, "I have serious doubts about this present marital union, to say nothing of its future."

"Oh, it's fine. Peter's an excellent golfer. He was an All-American in college. He wanted to play the Irish courses, and I wanted to see the country." She shrugged her shoulders. "It's worked out fine. We've had a wonderful time. Our last stop is Dublin, and then we're headed home."

"To be honest, I'm delighted that he's out whacking a golf ball round the countryside. Look what I'd have missed."

Trish smiled and sipped her drink.

The lounge was beginning to clear. The barman opened the front door to ease the stuffiness and clear the pall of cigarette smoke that clung to the ceiling. Brian collected two barstools and ordered another round. They sat facing each other, which allowed the occasional graze of a knee.

The conversation filled easily with talk of college days, spring breaks, Trish's interest in Joyce, and her hiking expeditions through Oregon. She had heard of Charles Parnell, the legendary Irish nationalist, but not of his affair with Kitty O'Shea, the wife of one of his supporters. Brian related the circumstances of the scandal, which destroyed Parnell's reputation and ended an extraordinary political career that many had assumed would bring him to the prime minister's office. As Brian finished the tale, a smile crossed her face.

"Boring you, am I?" he asked.

"Not at all. I thought it was a wonderful story. It just occurred to me this was the first conversation I've had in ten days that wasn't about golf."

Her insistence that the next round of drinks would be on her met token resistance.

"So here you are, an American in Dublin," she said. "How did that happen? Dark eyes, black hair. You have the black Irish look."

"Yeah, those Spanish traders were a pretty randy bunch back in the day."

"So, what brought you to Ireland? Have family?"

"Not really. At least, not that I know of. I'm doing a fellowship in Irish studies at University College Dublin. Six months to go."

When he mentioned his research had taken him to Paris, Trish said her plan after college had been to spend a year in France, immerse herself in the culture, do some writing, and travel around the continent. She had taken a minor in French and was reasonably fluent in the language. "Something I've always dreamed of doing." She paused. "But it's not likely to happen now."

"That's too bad. You'd have a great time."

She shrugged her shoulders. "So, Brian you're enjoying yourself, I presume."

"I am indeed. Having a fine time. Love the country."

"And have you found yourself a little Irish colleen?"

Brian shook his head. "Not really. I can't afford a girlfriend. You might say I only flirt with poverty." He grinned. "As a matter of fact ...." He leaned toward her, brought his lips to her ear. "It might become necessary," he whispered, "to vacate these premises prematurely, due to the sorry state of my finances."

Trish laughed. "Wouldn't that would be a great story. Me running from the law on my first visit to Dublin."

She turned to survey the nearly empty lounge. A boy was clearing ashtrays, bottles, and drink glasses from tables spaced along a maroon cushioned couch. In the cul-de-sac adjoining the entrance, three young couples, stylishly turned out, were sharing a bottle of white wine. One of the men had a Trinity College crew scarf casually draped over his shoulders. At the near end of the couch a young couple, pints of stout untouched, bent toward each other in conversation, occasionally putting down their cigarettes to hold hands. Just beyond, an older gentleman with a small whiskey on the table in front of him was reading *The Irish Times*, the smoke from his pipe trailing its edges.

Trish turned back to Brian. "I'm going to miss it."

"Miss what?" he asked.

"Oh, sitting in a bar with a stranger, getting a little mellow and curious, enjoying the tease."

Brian nodded toward the rings on her finger.

"Please understand," she said, "I love Peter. I'm just not used to that married feeling yet."

"So, what was the rush?"

Trish sighed. "Oh, a lot of things. Peter was offered a job in Florida where he could work on his golf game year around. He wanted me with him. We had been engaged for about three months and had vaguely spoken of marriage – you know, like something that would happen someday. But then he started asking, 'Why not now? We're going to do it anyway.' The families got involved, a momentum developed, and . . . here I am."

Brian nodded his understanding.

"It's funny," she continued, "but already there's a different feeling between Peter and me. It's not like it was when we were single, when we'd go away for a weekend . . . you know, the excitement, the sex we weren't supposed to be having, the romance. Since we've become legal something has changed, the spark isn't there, at least not like it used to be."

"Sounds like the honeymoon's over."

"I don't know. But I do know Peter's a good man." Trish was quiet for a moment, sipping her drink, her attention elsewhere, as though debating whether to change the personal tack of the conversation. She put her glass on the counter and turned to Brian. "I guess it's a strange thing to say but I don't know if I'm ready for a good man. I think I needed a few more notches on my belt, a rascal or two in my past, had my heart broken a few times. Perhaps then I'd appreciate what I've got. And wouldn't mind as much the long slog that seems – at least when you're twenty-three so… forever."

"A normal reaction, I'd imagine," Brian replied. "I'm sure every new bride has their second thoughts. It all works out in the end." He leaned forward, taking her hands in his. "But, I've got to say, you are one fine-looking bit of goods, as they say over here. And Peter's one lucky boyo."

"Thank you. I'm enjoying your company too. But see? This is what I mean. I need something, maybe a good kick in the ass, to make me realize I'm not single anymore."

"Not to worry, Trish. We're just ships in the night. A couple of people who shared a conversation one afternoon in a Dublin bar. And it was good fun."

"It was." She pulled her hands away and drew in a deep breath as if to collect herself. "I'm leaving, Brian."

"Just like that? When's Peter back?"

"Not until later. But I'm a little drunk." She smiled. "From the drinks that were hardly anything at all. I need something to eat."

"I know a bar, Sinnots, a block away. The best sandwiches in Dublin."

She shook her head. "I'm going back to the hotel. Need to sober up."

"Where are you staying?"

"The Shelbourne."

"Oh, one of Dublin's finest. Parnell and Kitty used to meet there, you know."

Trish reached for her sunglasses.

"One question, Trish. If I were to knock on your door with a bit of food and drink, would you turn me away?"

She stood up quickly. "Brian, thank you. I've really enjoyed meeting you. We'll leave it at that." She leaned over and kissed him on the cheek.

Heading toward the door, Trish stopped, steadied herself against the bar and put on her sunglasses. She turned once to wave and was gone.

The room was at the end of an empty corridor. The pattern at the center of a long stretch of carpet had worn away. Lithographs of country scenes hung at intervals along the wall. The young lady at the reception desk had been only too happy to supply the room number to an Irish cousin.

There was no response to his tentative knock, nor to the more forceful ones. Brian was about to turn away when he heard movement inside the room. The door opened. Trish seemed neither surprised nor upset to see him. She was barefoot, drying her hands on a white towel. The ends of her belt dangled from the loops of her unbuttoned khakis.

"Brian, I told you –"

He raised his arms. In one hand was a bottle of wine, a paper bag in the other. "As promised," he said, "food and drink."

Trish shook her head no.

"You have to eat something, so why not with me?" he asked. "And the wine is a rare vintage. Don't let the screw cap fool you."

She smiled and turned back into the room. Brian followed.

A fan turned slowly on the ceiling. Sunlight, filtered between half-opened drapes, brightened a portion of the four-poster bed centered on one wall. Four leather bags lay open on the floor, clothes spilling from each. Two golf clubs were propped in one corner.

Brian put the sandwiches and wine on the hall table and sat next to Trish on the bed.

"A little picnic, Trish. How does that sound?"

She shook her head. "No, whatever we're going to do, Brian, we have to do now, while I still have this buzz." She turned to him and smiled. "Before I lose my curiosity."

"In that case, our feast can wait. Fine with me." Brian took off his jacket and began unbuttoning his shirt.

Trish stood, shook out the loose braid from her hair, unbuttoned and shrugged off the Oxford; she placed her earrings and watch in the ashtray on the bedside table. Holding onto Brian's shoulder for support, she wiggled out of her khakis, kicked them across the room. Bra and panties – a matching light blue – taut over breasts and a delightfully shaped bottom were all that remained.

"Don't stop now, Trish. You're looking better all the time."

"That's your job, Brian. I like to leave some clothes on for the man. Especially when he's all worked up, you know he can't wait to get at it. Ends up just pulling things off." She laughed. "I love it, my own little torture."

"I'm not there yet. But I'm working at it."

"I've noticed."

So it began. Without kisses. Without talk. She responded eagerly, but Brian sensed a reticence, a withholding. Her hands were flat and unmoving on his back, no stab of fingernails, no spurs of urgency. Even at the end, her body pressed hard against his, the stifled cries Trish managed seemed less than authentic, more scripted than of pleasure. There was no point trying to prolong what little glow there was; she was finished.

Brian turned and fell away. He watched the shimmer of sun widen and close on the ceiling in sway with the breeze – tinged with the smell of peat – parting the drapes. He idly wondered if Parnell ever stared at the same ceiling those years ago with Mrs. O'Shea.

More to break the silence and perhaps put a smile on her face, Brian, his voice light and teasing, said, "I hope Peter had as much fun this afternoon playing golf as I had playing with his wife." Before the words were out of his mouth, he knew it was spectacularly the wrong thing to have said at that moment.

He turned to look at her. She had covered her face with her hands and was sobbing. Tears seeped between her fingers, streaking her cheeks. Brian dabbed them with a corner of the sheet.

"Trish, it's okay. Everything's fine," he told her. "Remember, ships in the night. No one will ever know about this."

"I'll know," she whispered. "Jesus, on my goddamn honeymoon. What's wrong with me?"

"Nothing is wrong with you." He hesitated. "Maybe this is the kick in the ass you said you needed." He gave a soft laugh. "Could be you'll thank me one day."

"Maybe, but right now I want you to leave."

"Trish, please. I don't want to go with you sad like this."

"I'll deal with it myself. Just leave."

He dressed quickly. Trish had covered herself with a sheet, her face buried in a pillow.

Brian started toward the door, then stopped. "I know this isn't a good time, but would you happen to have a couple of pounds? You know, the wine and sandwiches?"

"Look in my handbag," she said, her voice muffled. "Take whatever you need."

There was a five-pound and two single-pound notes, along with change, in her purse. Brian hesitated for a second before putting the fiver in his pocket. *A little extra for my efforts,* he thought, *scoundrels don't come cheap.* He relieved the hall table of the wine and made his way to the door, which he quietly opened and as quietly closed behind him. He later thought he probably should have said goodbye.

The decision to have a beer was resolved with the announcement that the Eastern shuttle to Boston would be delayed forty-five minutes. Brian found a place at the end of the bar next to a man drinking a martini and staring intently at the TV. He ordered a beer and lit a cigarette.

"Sink the sonofabitch," Brian heard next to him. He looked at the man and then at the TV. A golf match was in progress. The camera was focused on a player preparing to putt. Spectators lined the green. Another golfer and his caddy stood on the green some distance away.

As the golfer circled the cup, looking at the line of his putt from various angles, the camera panned in for a closeup of a group at the side of the green. In the center was a tall fair-haired man with a golf visor pushed back from his forehead, a white tee behind his ear. One arm held a kindergarten-age child, the other was draped around an attractive blonde.

In an instant, Brian recognized her. Except for the cropped hair, there was no mistaking Trish and the wide-eyed, perky look of five years ago. The camera lingered on the young girl for a moment; as it tailed away the man turned and squeezed Trish's shoulder. She looked up at him and smiled. It seemed a happy smile.

Brian signaled the barman for a another beer, lit up a cigarette, and pushed back from the bar. The serendipity of the moment had startled him. He had often recalled that afternoon in Davy's, the drink, the flirting, the aftermath at the Shelbourne wondering how life had been for Trish and Peter. Apparently well if the television snippet could be believed.

The cameras provided an additional bit of information that day, revealing another souvenir of that Irish holiday: a beautiful young girl, her dark eyes crinkled with laughter, with a thatch of curly black hair, and a striking resemblance to a certain student of Irish history.

17

THE VOCATION

A T THE 6:45 A.M. MASS in the chapel of St. Joseph's Church, a tentative sun begins its creep over the dozen or so parishioners, inching onto the altar, rescuing the Blessed Mother from the shadows, brightening her smile and the purple cassock of the celebrant, a portly Father Lyons.

Among those in attendance is Liam Flynn, a gangling youth draped over a pew at the rear of the chapel. Liam, sixteen years old, is in his senior year at St. Raphael's Academy, an institution run by the Christian Brothers in Pawtucket, Rhode Island. His presence at Mass serves a twofold, though perhaps contradictory, purpose: it satisfies the persistent request of Brother Joseph, his homeroom teacher and a strong advocate for his vocation; and brings him in reasonable proximity to Mary French, a girl on whom he has had a crush for several months.

In a droning monotone Father Lyons hurries through the first Scriptural reading, a letter from Saint Paul to the Ephesians. Liam follows in his daily missal. Although the admonition it contains, "prepare yourself and act in a manner worthy of your vocation," is eerily appropriate, Liam is not sure if the call were to come he would welcome it. His gaze drifts to Mary at the far end of his pew. Profiled in the soft tones of morning, auburn hair ringing a white kerchief, hands clasped beneath her chin,

Mary – the prettiest girl Liam has ever seen – kneels in prayer. *Now that,* David thinks, *is something worth praying for.*

When he made his pact with Brother Joseph, Liam indicated up front his lack of interest in becoming a religious but did agree, after much discussion, to prayerfully reflect on the possibility. Brother feels that a significant number of students – 10 per cent he often cites – are so blessed, many of whom are unaware of their designation. Daily Mass with communion and weekly confession complete Liam's end of the bargain. If, after an appropriate trial period it becomes apparent Liam's not one of the chosen, Brother will curtail his requests and not press the issue further.

His romantic aspirations regarding Mary French – a senior At St. Xavier's Academy in Providence, R. I. – are meager. An occasional smile or glance in his direction is all he needs. His imagination can do the rest. Liam has never spoken to Mary nor she to him. This level of unfamiliarity he considers an advantage. His appearance – skinny, bony face speckled with eruptions, an unruly thicket of hair, teeth in need of attention – is an image best viewed from afar. Such strategy also spares him the possibility of rejection.

The weeks pass. A month of consistent Mass attendance, innumerable prayers of petition, and weekly confession hasn't yielded anything resembling a calling – a result, Liam reasons, places him squarely in the ninety percent bracket. He decides to speak with Brother Joseph about his lack of progress. After classes that afternoon he asks Brother if he would meet with him for a few minutes.

"Of course, Liam. Just give me a moment." Brother is shuffling through two stacks of papers on his desk. He appears disheveled: white collar angled to the side, chalk dust sprinkled on the front and arms of his black habit, right hand stained with ink. The framed countenance of the order's founder, St. John De La Salle, benignly observes from his perch above the blackboard.

In a few minutes Brother pushes back from his desk. "So, Liam, how are things going?"

Liam describes his month-long effort, his adherence to the stipulations of their deal and the absence of anything that might be considered a sign of a vocation.

Brother listens intently. and with a smile responds, "Liam, you remind me so much of myself at your age: so incredibly impatient and naïve." He points to the blackboard behind him filled with equations. "Do you think you can understand algebra in a few weeks? More like a few months before it begins to make sense." He stands, brushes chalk dust from his vestments, approaches Liam and takes his hands in his. "You're not to worry, my friend. God is testing your resolve, your patience. He's not only the captain of your soul, but the captain of the ship that takes you through life. If you decide to sail with Him, be part of His crew, you must be seaworthy, able for the storms and rocky shoals that lie ahead. This is all preparation for the grand journey that awaits you. It's not meant to be easy." Brother Joseph frequently speaks in this manner.

"But how will I know, Brother?"

"You'll know, Liam." His voice softens. "Think of your calling as a seedling which one day suddenly blossoms. And with it comes an unimaginable peace, a serenity – and a certainty – that only God can provide."

Liam persists. "What if it doesn't happen?"

"We accept that as God's decision." Brother Joseph joins his hands together as in prayer. "Let's hope that won't be the case."

A September morning two weeks later, Mass in the chapel begins uneventfully. This inhospitable space – severe, unpainted walls, plain glass windows nailed shut, absent statues (other than the Blessed Mother) or pleasing ornamentation, its stale air laced with musty remnants of summer – was created to accommodate the spillover from Sunday liturgies in the main church. Mary French is in her usual place: head bowed, rosary beads dangling from her clasped hands. Father Lyons moves quickly through the liturgy; his morning Mass never exceeds twenty minutes.

As the Consecration approaches, Liam puts aside his missal to read a prayer card given to him by Brother Joseph entitled, "A Young Man's

Prayer For Guidance." Seconds after finishing its three paragraphs, Liam experiences a peculiar sensation. A warm flush, like an intense sunburn, passes through him, followed by shaking chills. His head begins to throb. Sweat forms on his forehead. His belly tightens. For a moment he thinks he might be sick.

Not sure what to do, Liam leans forward and puts his head on the back of the facing pew. *What's happening?* he wonders. Although some Italian spices have caused similar problems in the past, he hasn't had any lately. Plus, he felt fine getting up this morning. His head bent, he gradually begins to feel better. With it comes a curious sense of contentment, a calming bliss – his mind clear and uncluttered, as though vacuumed of debris. *Could this be the Holy Spirit entering me, preparing me?* he wonders. *Is this the peace Brother talked about?* The more he considers the circumstances – occurring during Mass, at the consecration no less, just after finishing the prayer for guidance – the more certain he becomes of its spiritual origin. When he lifts his head, Mary French is watching him. A look of concern crowds her pretty face.

The unusual feelings persist through the day. At the end of class, he mentions to Brother Joseph the possibility of a calling. Brother listens carefully to his story. When Liam concludes, Brother breaks into a broad grin.

"Liam," he exclaims, "God does work in mysterious ways, does he not? I pray for all my students, but always added some extra Aves for you. And it looks like it worked! Congratulations."

Liam wonders out loud if it's too early to consider it a real vocation. Brother Joseph waves away his concerns. "The seed that was planted has broken ground," he responds, his tone exultant. "Now, with care and nourishment, it will grow and mature."

Brother Joseph is the youngest of the congregation at St. Raphael's. Liam guesses he's in his mid-twenties, although a sixteen-year-old's judgment of age might be faulty. To Liam, Brother Joseph epitomizes a truly religious person, both in behavior and appearance. His deep-set eyes and hollowed face, a shade or two darker than his starched white collar, resembles those of the frail ascetics in Liam's religion book. A full head of black hair, cropped unevenly, spreads across his forehead. Conversations with him – kindness inflected in each syllable – frequently reference God, the Blessed Mother, and various Saints. Liam can't imagine being that holy. And he also wonders how Brother could be so sure of his vocation. To commit his whole life to a mysterious, unseen God requires a faith that has eluded Liam. Maybe today will change all that.

"Come," Joseph continues. "We must tell Brother Vincent."

The principal, Brother Vincent, is more reserved, offering only occasional comments as he listens to Liam's story. He does agree that a potential vocation must be considered, and he mentions a two-day retreat scheduled in three weeks at the Christian Brothers Novitiate in Barrytown, New York. Young men considering the Christian Brothers as a career choice are invited to attend after obtaining parental permission. Liam asks both brothers to keep his plans confidential for the moment.

Expressing an interest in becoming a Brother allows an additional benefit: improvement in grades. Liam stumbles on this revelation by chance.

Jimmy Messier, a classmate, declared his vocation the previous year. His decision took many by surprise; Jimmy doesn't resemble the typical candidate. Older than his classmates, he smokes, wears "flashy" clothes, and has an abundance of black hair swept into a DA (duck's ass). More significantly, he drives a convertible with California mufflers, and girls are occasionally spotted in the passenger seat. He and Liam sit next to each other in class and have become friendly. The day after his conversation with the principal, Liam casually asks Jimmy what prompted his decision to become a brother.

"Between the two of us, okay?"

"Agreed," Liam answers.

"When I failed French and Algebra last year, my father told me I had to pass high school before I could take over the family business, a gas station." Jimmy had heard about the generous grades that come the way of those who declare a vocation. "So I did."

"And it worked?" Liam asks.

"Still here, ain't I?"

"So you're not going to be a Brother?"

"You gotta be kidding. I'm not that stupid."

"So what will you do?"

"As soon as I know I'm going to graduate, I'll lose my vocation. I'll be sad and tearful, but what are they going to say?"

And that's exactly what Jimmy Messier does.

A few days later, Liam breaks the news of the retreat to his family, a tight Irish Catholic cohort. The reaction is mixed, enthusiasm for the trip dividing along gender lines.

His paternal grandfather, an émigré from Ireland in the 1870s, died a few years earlier, but Liam remembers the intensity of his faith. A fourth-degree Knight of Columbus and daily communicant after retiring from the mill, whose pockets were never absent rosary beads, he would have been ecstatic about his grandson's decision.

Liam's father is similarly inclined. Also a Knight of Columbus, he spent two years at La Salette Seminary studying for the priesthood. For reasons never made clear, he left the seminary, but his devotion to the Church remains rock solid. "That's fantastic," he responds, eager to learn the details.

On the distaff side, his paternal grandmother – a dominant, intimidating presence – and Liam's mother have similar personalities and mind sets. They also are devout Catholics. Church edicts are adhered to; Sunday Mass, feast days, and holy days of obligation are scrupulously observed. Respect for priests and nuns is sincere and unwavering. Tithes are adequate and contributed punctually.

However, neither consider becoming a priest, brother, or other religious a worthy endeavor. They fall short of saying those answering the call are people unable to make it in the real world, but comments over the years hint at that perception. An analogy they would agree with: the skier who finds himself on a challenging slope, rather than hanging tough, finds an escape trail and bails out. Success in business, politics, or having a government job is their definition of success. In his grandmother's memory, the person she most admired is not one of the Church hierarchy, to include the Pope, but Franklin D. Roosevelt. Given this background, their reactions are predictable.

Grandma doesn't comment. His mother's "Oh, that's nice," sums up her enthusiasm. Nothing comparable to their delight when he makes the honor roll. Permission to attend the retreat is given. His mother's concern is who will do the paper route. "I'll tell you right now," she adds, "it won't be me."

On a Thursday morning in October, two vans, each with six young men aboard, leave Rhode Island. Approximately five hours later, they are winding along a rain-slicked road in New York's Hudson River Valley. Their destination: the village of Barrytown, now moments away.

None of the group has traveled these roads before. All are familiar, however, with the bewitched region Washington Irving described in *The Legend of Sleepy Hollow*. On this gray afternoon – leaves scurrying as they pass, smatters of rain on the windshield, the smudge of misted hamlets along the way – some of the more imaginative of the group could be forgiven their occasional glimpse of a headless horseman.

The novitiate, enclosed by an iron link fence attached to stone pillars, is centered by a large brick structure solemn and imposing under the overcast sky. Five or six smaller structures complete the compound.

With the help of a novice – a young man in training to become a brother – Liam locates his room. The furnishings are sparse: two cots, a light fixed to the head of each, a wood dresser missing drawer handles, a closet, and two chairs next to a square table. Above the door is a tilted crucifix, at its side a dry holy water font. The bathroom and showers are located midway down the corridor.

His roommate arrives; introductions are made. Sal is from Queens, New York, with an accent to match. Shorter than Liam, with a swarthy, partially bearded face, curly black hair, and a tattoo peeking beneath a rolled-up shirt cuff, he reminds Liam of Jimmy Messier – their looks more pool hustler than aspiring religious. Sal looks around the room. "Jeez, is this it?" His tone is softened by a grin lined with white, even teeth. Bunks chosen, he departs. "Goodbyes to attend to. Catch you later."

That evening, the students assemble in a hall on the first floor of the main building. The retreat master, Brother Cyril – a ruddy-faced, older man – addresses them, holding a crucifix in his left hand.

"Welcome, gentlemen," he begins. "Before I outline your schedule and touch on some of the ground rules, I want to make an important point." He pauses. "We at the novitiate did not invite you young men here so we might badger you about your vocation or pressure you into becoming a Christian Brother. Rather, these two days are meant as an introduction to our community and way of life. We want you to understand our mission, its goals, and the operation we've put in place to accomplish them, and specifically the preparation required of those who will, if so blessed, join us in our endeavor. We presently have fifteen novices in training, and we encourage you to chat with them and share their experiences." His smile is disarming. "Now, with that out of the way: welcome to our home. We are delighted to have you as our guests."

Brother Cyril then outlines the schedule and restrictions: Mass is mandatory and celebrated at 7:00 a.m. Breakfast follows. Mornings are devoted to lectures and group discussions. Students will receive a schedule. Afternoons are loosely structured. Various sports activities are available, along with hikes along the Hudson River. Afternoon devotions, non-compulsory, are held in the chapel at 4:00 p.m. The angelus announces supper, after which there is a series of informal group discussions. Other than Mass, attendance is not taken, and no grades will be assigned at the close of the retreat. Lights out at 10:00 p.m. Smoking is permitted outside the buildings; alcohol is not allowed.

At supper the first evening, two novices sit at each of the tables, available for questions. During the meal, students are invited to stand, introduce themselves, and tell something of their background and what decided them to attend the retreat.

At age sixteen, Liam is told he is one of the youngest in the group. He is also one of the tallest. Five inches have been added to his five-foot, six-inch frame of a year ago. Although pleased with his height, he feels awkward, adopting a slump when standing before a seated group, such as this evening. His remarks are brief, dealing only with essentials: name, address and year in school. "I don't know for sure if I have a vocation," he adds. "Brother Joseph, my homeroom teacher, says that coming here will open my eyes and make me more certain. He also says to pray hard, which I will do while I'm here. Thank you." There are a few claps as he sits down.

As the introductions continue, the pious, rosy-cheeked altar-boy types he expected do not materialize. All seem surprisingly normal.

Sal offers only his name and hometown. Later, in their room, he adds some background. He lives in the "tough" section of Queens, part of a large, third-generation immigrant Sicilian family. His father and uncles work in a variety of nonspecific jobs that are profitable. His mother is very religious. Her wish – as long as Sal can remember – is that one of her four sons have a religious vocation. This, she insists, was the wish of her mother as she lay close to death. Over the years there have been concerted efforts – novenas, devotions, Masses, candles in front of statues all around their home – to have the family so honored. His three older brothers are not in contention; a boyfriend, an unexpected birth, and a jail sentence removed them from the running. His mother's plea – "Just do it for Grandma, God rest her soul, and me who raised you," she pauses, "while there's still time" – is becoming more insistent.

"So, Liam, I'm doing this retreat to please my mother," he concludes, "get her off my back, and then maybe we can blow out some of those damn candles before the house burns down."

The room lights begin blinking, announcing 10:00 p.m.

"But the real problem is, there's this girl. You got a girlfriend, Liam?"

"No, not really." *There's Mary French*, he thinks. *But how can she be a girlfriend when I've never spoken to her?*

"Then you wouldn't understand."

Liam goes to the bathroom to brush his teeth. Returning, he pushes open the door. Sal is kneeling by the side of his bed, head bent, saying his prayers. Liam stands quietly until he finishes, not wishing to embarrass him.

Thinking about the episode later, Liam realizes Sal isn't one to be easily embarrassed. Being seen on his knees wouldn't concern him in the slightest. Unlike his roommate, who is afraid of being made fun of and imagines snickers behind his back, Sal puts his faith out there for anyone to see, without thinking twice. Liam is the one who should be embarrassed – and he is.

The following morning brings clear skies, brisk air, and a warm sun. The grass and foliage are wet and glistening from the previous night. The novitiate, dark and dismal when first encountered, is scarcely improved by the light of day. A stolid, square fortress, it has, other than sturdiness, little style to offer. John D. Rockefeller built and presented it to the brothers as part of a land swap for property owned by the order that adjoined his property in Tarrytown.

With an hour free, Sal and Liam decide to explore the property. A short walk brings them to a dense grove of trees, and in single file they follow a path cleared of brush. Gusts of wind whistle through the taller pines; damp ground smells of mold. Sal leads the way; there is a swagger in his gait: weight forward, rolling his shoulders like a movie tough guy. After a few minutes they reach a clearing on the crest of a hill.

Spread before them is a picturesque range of blue-shadowed hills and shallow valleys. A breeze blows clean and fresh. Broad fields, some scattered with heaps of corn stalks, others untilled, stretch on either side. Groves of trees – their leaves late-autumn dull – are scattered about. Just beyond winds the majestic Hudson. Way off, dusky in the distance, are the Catskills.

Below where they are standing are four stone-walled fields, in the center of which are two barns, some chicken coops, two pigs in a muddy pen and a silo. Cows graze in two of the fields, another has been harvested and one lies fallow.

"Must be the Brothers' farm," Liam remarks.

"You know, Liam, this is the first real farm I've ever seen in my life. Lots of pictures, but never the real thing."

"You really are a city boy," Liam says, laughing.

"And another thing. You'll get a kick out of this. I have never before been in such a silent place. Except maybe a bird chirping once in a while and us talking, there's no sound here."

"Never thought about it, but you're right."

"Where I live, there's always noise. Nonstop. Even if you wake up in the middle of the night, you hear cars, police sirens, subways going by, people fighting next door, voices on the street." He shakes his head. "Here it's really – what's the word – serene. You know, maybe this is where you go when you die. If you're really good."

"In that case, buddy, I won't be seeing you there.."

Sal explodes with a laugh, white teeth sparkling. "You're probably right."

The next afternoon the students are invited to sit in on various classes. "Morality and the Crusades: Advocating war in the name of religion" is the topic being discussed in Liam's group.

The speaker describes the greed and corruption that characterized the nine expeditions, as well as the thousands of innocent lives lost, initiated with questionable intent in the name of God. The Popes involved are not spared the speaker's scathing review. The forty-five minutes pass quickly.

One of the novices, a tall, burly guy with a crop of red hair, departs the classroom at the same time as Liam. His body fills the door frame.

"You play football in high school?" Liam asks.

"Yup, linebacker and wide receiver."

They exchange first names. Liam, after some small talk, asks Pete about his decision to join the Brothers and how's it working out.

"Well, I probably shouldn't tell you this, seeing as you're thinking about joining us. My decision had nothing to do with religion or being holy."

"I'm not especially holy, either," Liam replies. "So how did it happen?"

"It started with football. I was a pretty good player, but not good enough for scholarships, plus my grades were in the toilet. Our football coach has a son who was a helluva football player, could have gotten a free ride at a half-dozen places. Blowing his father's mind, he goes off and becomes a Christian Brother.

"One day the coach and I get talking, and he says I should try it. He's seen me with my family at church and was thinking it might suit me. 'I go because I have to,' I tell him. 'Plus, I like girls.' So what,' he tells me. 'My son, the Brother, does too.'"

"Anyway, long story short, I came on a retreat like you and pretty much fell in love with the place. I'm still not very religious, don't buy a lot of that supernatural crap."

"So when do you finish here?"

"Another year."

"What will you do after that?"

"I want to teach. The Brothers tell me I have a natural ability. I've taken a lot of extra science courses. I want to be a missionary and teach kids science. You don't need an advanced degree for where I want to go."

"So," Liam asks, "how about the girls?"

Pete's smile is as wide as his shoulders. "Before I committed, I threw myself into women for about three months. Went through 'em like Sherman went through Georgia. And you know what? I like what I'm doing here more than what I did with them."

That night after supper, a service is held in the chapel in recognition of the student visitors and to bless their intentions. Once the students are seated, the novices – each wearing a white surplice – proceed to their places at the side of the sanctuary. One of their group lights the altar candles; shadows chase down the windowless walls. Thick, gray smoke spilling from a gold incense holder on the altar stings the eyes.

The Retreat Master Brother Cyril and the novitiate director are seated in two large, red-embroidered chairs. Cued by a violin, the novices stand to sing what Liam later learns is a Gregorian chant. The ancient Latin verses plod along without inflection, a stark contrast to the youthful voices.

In his remarks, Brother Cyril thanks all for attending and hopes the experience offers a clearer understanding of what the Christian Brothers are about. His hope and prayer is that some among them will consider joining the organization. An invitation to visit the novitiate at any time, for any reason, is extended.

In closing, he adds, "Let me leave you with what I think is the best advice I can give young people: whatever road you find yourself on in life – be it bumpy, smooth, rutted, filled with detours and dead ends, or taking you in the wrong direction – always keep in touch with your Maker. Talk to Him. Talk to Him every day. Chat as you would with a friend. He's always on call. He will always listen. And, my friends, He will work wondrous things in your life." Brother Cyril pauses. "God bless you all. When you head off tomorrow afternoon, may your trip be safe."

The notes of an organ resound through the Chapel. A novice stands. With a clear, unwavering falsetto he begins the "Ave Maria." The other novices join him, their voices muted to a hum. The organ accompanies, not with crashing chords, but single, plaintive notes pitched an octave above the singer's voice. In the semi-darkness, a splendid hymn filling the space, candles flickering, shadows darting, incense wafting, the effect is surreal. Liam glances at his roommate. Sal sits rigid as a statue, hands clasped, in rapt attention. With the final soaring crescendo, the choir at full throat, the organist letting out all the stops – it's a goosebump moment.

Two or three students stand and applaud. They are quickly joined by the rest. "What do you think, Sal?" Liam asks.

Sal doesn't answer, only shakes his head, a look of wonder on his face.

That night, lying in bed talking back and forth across the room, Liam tells Sal the football player's story.

"Yeah," Sal agrees, "it's great and good for him. But I don't know if I could do it. I got this girlfriend I really like. Since I told her I was coming here, she thinks there's something wrong with her, not putting out enough or something. I tell her she's great. Now she thinks I might be queer."

"Really?"

"Not really, but it bothers me. Like tonight, Friday, we always take in a movie, then afterwards go parking someplace." As Sal describes her and what they do together, his breathing becomes heavier, his voice thicker. He begins thrashing about as though the bed's uncomfortable.

"You okay, Sal?"

A long few seconds later, he responds, "Yeah, yeah, I'm fine. See you in the morning." Soon all is heard are gentle snores from his side of the room.

As Liam waits for sleep to kick in, he marvels at all he's learned this day – and that's not even counting the Crusades.

The following morning, another autumn beauty, the visitors prepare for a noon departure. The four students joining Sal and Liam for breakfast agree with them that it was a great couple of days. Of the group only one believes the experience finalized his decision to become a Brother. Three of the others feel it wasn't a game changer but did offer a lot to think and pray about. Liam allies himself with that camp. Sal is non-committal offering only a wise guy smirk.

On schedule the van for Rhode Island arrives and within minutes they are ready for departure. Just before pulling out of the parking lot, the driver decides to make a bathroom visit. With that accomplished, and novices waving from the novitiate steps, the van pulls away.

The return route goes through the village of Barrytown. A high school football game has just ended, and spectators are streaming down a street toward the van, now stopped at a corner. A policeman is directing traffic. Among those approaching is a trio of cheer leaders wearing short red skirts and white sweaters inscribed Barrytown High. Nearing the corner, one of the cheerleaders drops her pompom. As she bends to retrieve it, a gust of wind lifts her skirt, bringing into view a creamy expanse of thigh and a flash of light blue panties. She straightens quickly, and with pompom in hand, crosses the street. Like a crack of lightning across the night sky, the whole episode lasts but a few seconds, just long enough for the breeze that lifted her skirt to run off with Liam's vocation. A sudden throb punctuates the certainty of this realization, bringing with it a sense of relief.

During the trip back to Rhode Island, Liam reviews the retreat. The brothers did a great job, he thinks, transforming what he assumed would be two days of prayer, religious services, and vocation counseling into a low-key getaway with sports activities, interesting discussions, and a good bunch of guys. He debates how to approach Brother Joseph: tell him he is still unsure about his vocation, or be honest and let him know the finality of his decision? Liam feels it best not to inform Brother Joseph that the verdict came about not as a result of reflection, but rather serendipity. If the van driver hadn't decided to relieve himself when he did, the van wouldn't have been at the corner the precise moment the gust spun through – and maybe his story would have a different ending.

Before class the following Monday, Brother Joseph is eager to hear about the retreat. "Tell me all about it. Everything went well?"

Liam assures him that everything went very well and that he enjoyed it thoroughly. He mentions how helpful the Brothers were, the valuable insights the novices provided, and how inspiring the liturgy. He describes the rooms ("Just the same as when I was there," Brother Joseph remarks) and some of the physical changes that are being made on the grounds ("About time").

"And you, Liam?" Joseph interjects. "Did it strengthen your resolve?"

Liam fidgets, shifting from one foot to the other, wishing the bell would sound to start class. "Certainly, Brother, it's a wonderful calling. The last two days have made me appreciate the wonderful work the Brothers do. But . . ." he hesitates. "I just don't feel I have the strength to lead that holy a life – you know, the poverty, chastity, and obedience part. I don't think I could do them all. You see, Brother, I have a weakness."

Brother Joseph pauses to collect his thoughts. His expectant smile is gone, his face now creased with concern. "Liam, we all have our weaknesses. God knows I do. Prayer and penance provide me the grace to keep wayward impulses at bay. So don't think you're alone in this."

"I know, but the difference between us, Brother . . . some of the impulses I don't want to keep away. I want to try them out. I'm only sixteen. Maybe in a couple of years I'll change my mind. But not now." He pauses. "I'm sorry. I know you had great hopes for me."

Brother Joseph shakes his head. "Don't be sorry, Liam. Of course I'm disappointed. I wanted you and me to be one with Christ. But you tried. There's nothing more either I or the Lord can ask."

The class bell finally rings. "One last thing, Liam. Remember when I told you that God is the captain of your ship?"

"Yes, Brother."

"Well, that ship has many passengers, many destinations, many ports to sink its anchor. And not everyone gets off at the same place. Many sail a long time before they find where they belong, their haven. Thank God I've found mine. I pray you find yours."

"Thank you, Brother."

They remain friends. Brother Joseph never mentions the vocation again.

As a result of his decision, Liam's presence at morning Mass is less consistent. The times he does attend, Mary French is there. She now sits on his side of the middle aisle; he's not sure if that's a good sign or not. She seems more devout than ever: shoulders caved, head bowed, intent on her rosary. The glances in his direction are less frequent, and when they do occur, they're more of a wide-eyed stare, looking but not seeing. Even her smiles, which used to have a hint of friendliness, now seem fixed, as though painted on.

Senior year is winding down; a college is chosen. As Liam looks back on his three years of high school, he acknowledges some success: honor roll most of the time, second string on the basketball team. But his social life has been a disaster. A few parties and the occasional dance pretty much cover it. In an attempt at redemption, and while there's still an opportunity, Liam decides to attend the senior prom.

To his surprise, everyone at home is supportive, especially his mother. The choice of a partner for the occasion, however, is a challenge. He has no one to ask. Some of his friends have sisters who could probably be talked into going.

After considerable thought and sleep-disturbing anxiety, Liam makes his choice: Mary French. After years of quick glances and sly smiles, it's time to give it a go. He'll be forever kicking himself if he lets this last chance to meet her slip away.

The telephone rings at the French residence a half-dozen times. No answer. The receiver falls from Liam's moist hand to the floor. His right hand holds a piece of paper. In the distance he hears, "Hello, hello." He retrieves the receiver.

"Hello. You don't know me." He speaks rapidly. "My name is Liam Flynn. Is Mary there?"

"No, I'm her mother. Can I take I take a message?"

"Well," Liam blurts, "I would like to take you – I mean Mary – to the senior prom at St. Raphael Academy. The date is June sixth. It's being held at" – he turns over the sheet of paper he is reading from – "the Rhodes Ballroom."

There is a soft laugh at the other end of the phone. "I know who you are, Liam. Mary spoke of you frequently."

"She did?"

"Yes, she was hoping you would talk to her, but you never did. In any case, Mary won't be going to the prom."

"Well, that's fine, Mrs. French. I just thought I'd try."

"She won't because she's not here. She entered the convent – Sisters of Mercy – about a month ago."

Liam pauses for a long moment, then says, "I had no idea." He isn't sure if he should be happy or sad. Anyway, he's not so nervous. The pressure's off.

"I chuckled, Liam, because you're part of the reason she's there."

"Me?"

"Yes. She heard you were going to become a Brother, and that got her thinking more seriously about her own vocation. That is one of the reasons she wanted to talk to you."

"As a matter of fact, Mrs. French, I'm not going to be a Brother. I've lost my vocation."

"Oh, that's too bad. I'll let Mary know."

"Would it be okay if I tell her myself? Send her a letter?"

"That would be fine."

Liam copies the address and, about to say goodbye, asks how Mary is doing at the convent.

"Fine, I guess. We're only allowed one phone call a week. Even mail is restricted during the probation period." She pauses. "You know, Liam, I wish she'd waited a little longer. I tried to get her to. Just six months, even. But no, she's so set in her thinking, so intense, so . . . I can't think of the word to describe her."

"Determined?" Liam volunteers

"More than that. It will come to me. Anyway, Liam, I enjoyed our – fervent," she interjects. "That's the word. Her fervor, especially her devotion to the Blessed Mother. It's like a fire inside her. It frightens me sometimes. But I guess I should be happy. It's such a wonderful calling. Write to her, Liam."

"I will. When you're talking with her, please give her my address, 22 Denver Street, in case she would like to get in touch with me. Thank you. Goodbye, Mrs. French."

Liam does write to Mary. The letter is "returned to sender" two weeks later.

Graduation ceremonies are held in the school gym, decorated with class photos, trophies, and clusters of balloons. A banner over the stage reads *Congratulations Class of 1964*. The Bishop remains in attendance, having distributed the diplomas earlier with a firm handshake. Liam seeks out Brother Joseph to say his goodbyes. He finds him chatting with a young boy.

"Brother," Liam says, "before heading off I just want to thank you for your help over the years. You've been wonderful to me, and I'm very appreciative."

Brother Joseph's responses fit the occasion: how he enjoyed Liam's friendship, his wishes for success in college, and of course, the promise to keep him in his prayers. Liam listens to the words but senses Brother has moved on: The project that was Liam has been archived; his focus is now someplace else.

Brother Joseph introduces his young companion: a tousled-haired boy with wide blue eyes and fuzz on his upper lip. "Thomas will be with us next year," Brother Joseph says. "I'll be helping him during the summer to get ready for high school. A fair amount of work, but we'll have a good time, too. Right, Thomas?" Thomas nods yes. "But now we're going to have some cookies and soda."

Liam watches as they walk away: the boy walking stiffly, arms straight by his side, Joseph's hand on his shoulder, guiding him through the crowd.

Halfway through Liam's freshman year, the college experience must be, he decides, similar to what convicts feel when they are paroled from prison. Gone are the restrictions and restraints of home and high school; he's free now to do pretty much anything he wishes this side of the law. The Liam now and the younger version are, he feels, more like third cousins – related but with little else in common.

Liam is considering this one Friday afternoon while shaving for a party that night. *This time a year ago,* he thinks, *I would, perhaps, be getting ready to go to a movie that would have me home by ten o'clock – perhaps because it would depend on my last report card.* Curfew tonight will be decided by how well he handles his beer.

The image in the mirror has also changed. Extra pounds have filled out his face. The blemishes are gone, the long hair now stylishly cut. Braces have improved his smile. His height, so long camouflaged, now is flaunted.

Liam's improved appearance and sociability have brought him in contact with a heretofore little known and untouched population: girls. Successful encounters at bars and parties have improved his confidence. The rejection fears of high school are no longer: Replacements are so available, there's little time for dejection.

The folks at home are pleased; his grade average is good. They might be upset that the daily missal he brought with him has not yet seen the light of day or the interior of a church. It remains where it started – at the bottom of his suitcase.

One morning about six weeks later Liam receives two letters. The first is from Sal, saying he's going to another retreat at Barrytown, "just to listen to the silence again." Would Liam be interested in coming? The Friday night girlfriend is no longer. Seems she was seeing someone else all the while. "Let me know if you decide to join me."

Liam smiles. *Unless you can promise a cheerleader and a cooperative breeze, I think I'll pass.*

The second letter, forwarded by his father, is from Mary French. The first paragraphs recollect their mornings at Mass and the mutual shyness that prevented conversation. The reason for her letter: She heard he had been interested in the Christian Brothers but hadn't continued on to the novitiate. Her final vows are to occur in six months, and she has some serious concerns. Since he considered, then rejected, a vocation, she would like to hear his thoughts. She will be home during the first two weeks of April, and if he is around, "Could we meet?" The letter closes with, "God bless you, Liam. I hope you can help me." Then a P.S.: "I would have gladly gone to the prom with you."

Liam writes a brief note back saying he will be home, as the dates coincide with spring break. He promises to call her. His meager response tells the story. The infatuation for Mary, the pining that lasted the years of high school, feels as though it all never happened. Probably flew away with the same breeze that made light blue his favorite color. Now the chance to meet is more chore than anticipation.

Two days before the start of April vacation, Liam receives an invitation to join a group heading to Fort Lauderdale. Hundreds of college kids let loose, he is told, a non-stop party. He readily accepts.

Later that week, while sipping a Schlitz beer at a poolside pub and admiring the chest of the girl tending bar, Liam glances at her name tag. At that moment he remembers the promise he made to meet with Mary. The guilt passes quickly.

I'll call her when I get home, he figures, *and set up another time.* He never does.

A year later, Liam is told by a friend who also knew Mary that she did, in fact, take her final vows. The friend also mentions that four months later, on a bitterly cold Minnesota morning, she was found in the convent cemetery, lying before the beckoning arms of a snow-capped statue of the Virgin Mary, her hands clasped around her rosary, fingers frozen together. They were still together when she was placed in the ground.

About the Author

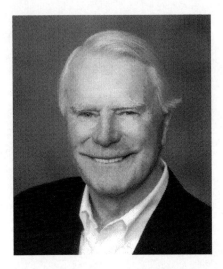

After graduation from the Royal College of Surgeons in 1961, Dr. McKee completed an internship and residency in Family Medicine at Memorial Hospital in Pawtucket, R.I. Then, fulfilling an ROTC commitment, he entered the US Air Force, and was assigned to the 551st USAF Hospital at Otis AFB on Cape Cod, Mass., as a General Medical Officer. Subsequently he was chosen to attend the School of Aerospace Medicine in San Antonio, Texas.

Upon completion of that program he returned to Otis AFB where he headed the Flight Surgeon's office. Discharged from active military duty in 1966, he joined the medical staff of United Airlines working in Denver; Washington, D.C.; and New York. (Dr. McKee maintained a military affiliation and retired, after twenty years of service, as Hospital Commander of the 143rd Airlift Wing, R. I. Air National Guard.)

Dr. McKee returned to R.I. in 1970 and established a family practice, became board-certified, and maintained the practice until 2000. During this time-span he also directed the occupational health program at the Electric Boat Division of General Dynamics in R.I.

Dr. McKee occupied a number of executive and clinical leadership positions at South County Hospital in Wakefield, R.I., and has enjoyed associations with various medical and civic organizations over the years.

He is a member of the R.I. Air National Guard Society, MENSA, and the R.I. Historical Society.

Dr. McKee was appointed Medical Director of an urgent care facility, a position he maintained until his retirement in 2013.

Married and the father of five, Dr. McKee resides in Narragansett, R.I. Author contact: genem1@cox.net

Other works by Gene McKee:

DOC

How a Reluctant Yank Found Himself
Becoming a Physician Among the Irish

Prodded by his formidable Aunt Bertha to become a doctor, college-grad Gene McKee, agrees to explore Europe in search of a welcoming medical school. Seizing the opportunity will provide relief from the tedium and stench of a temporary job as a fish cutter in Rhode Island.

The frustrations and apparent futility of the quest, extending through Ireland, England, Scotland, and France, test his resolve. But just before the clock's final tick, an unlikely acceptance to the Royal College of Surgeons in Dublin opens the door to a future not exactly of his own choosing.

McKee's rite-of-passage travelogue is replete with anecdotes of medical school and Dublin life during the late 1950s and early '60s. Recounted with self-deprecating humor and considerable honesty, we witness McKee's transformation from a reluctant medical student to a competent physician. Enjoyably peppered with historical tidbits, amorous entanglements, and imaginative riffs, reading *DOC* and seeing Ireland with its rich cast of "characters" through a young Irish-American's eyes, will surely bring smiles to the faces of readers and for some, a twinge of recognition.

DOC is available from Amazon, Barnes & Noble and from local bookstores everywhere.

BLOODLETTING TO BINARY

A Physician in a Small Hospital
in Rhode Island
An Extraordinary Era in American Medicine

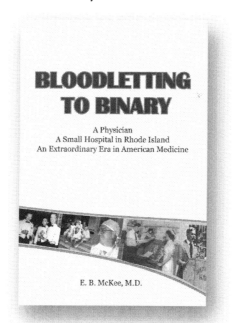

E. B. McKee's first book, *DOC*, chronicles adventures before, during, and after graduating from the prestigious Royal College of Surgeons in Ireland, in 1961. His self-deprecating and humorous style continues in *Bloodletting to Binary*. We rejoin McKee's medical journey upon his entrance into the USAF. In 1970, following his military discharge, with a wife, three children, and paltry bank balance, he establishes a private practice in southern Rhode Island.

McKee's career spans an era when medicine undergoes fundamental changes: from leeches to computer diagnostics, DNA testing, and robotic surgery. Vignettes capture South County Hospital's bare-bones beginnings: rudimentary X-ray capability, a borrowed EKG machine, and limited lab resources. Growth from a converted private home to the gleaming edifice that exists today is fondly recalled.

Hospital politics are on display. Watch the cadre of entrenched, older physicians circle the wagons to protect the status quo and slow the advance of specialist interlopers. Patients resist change too, fiercely loyal to the doctors who delivered their babies, performed their surgeries, set broken bones, and took care of their kids.

Bloodletting to Binary is a physician's behind-the-scenes story of irascible colleagues, hospital dramas, and unforgettable patients, while offering a snapshot of a transformational period in American medicine.

DOC and *Bloodletting to Binary* are both available from Amazon, Barnes & Noble and from local bookstores everywhere.

59968105R00117